THE FURTHEST STATION

THE FURTHEST STATION

BEN AARONOVITCH

This edition first published in Great Britain in 2018 by Gollancz

First published in Great Britain in 2017 by Gollancz
an imprint of the Orion Publishing Group Ltd
Carmelite House, 50 Victoria Embankment
London EC4Y 0DZ

An Hachette UK Company

1 3 5 7 9 10 8 6 4 2

A CIP catalogue record for this book is
available from the British Library.

ISBN 978 1 473 22243 4

Typeset by Input Data Services Ltd, Somerset

Printed in Great Britain by Clays Ltd, St Ives plc

www.gollancz.co.uk

To Bob Hunter, who still doesn't understand his role in making me look good.

Whoever you are, I have always depended on the kindness of strangers.

A Streetcar Named Desire, Tennessee Williams

1

Ceci n'est pas un métro

Jaget said he'd been watching this documentary on TV about the way people learn to track animals.

'Not white people, right?' he said. 'Like people that grow up in the bush.'

In this case !Xun people from Southern Africa, only Jaget couldn't do the click sound until I taught him. I can only do it because I once harboured romantic dreams of emigrating to South Africa and had got someone to teach me. Since I hadn't practised in ten years we were probably both doing it wrong. We got some funny looks from our fellow passengers – possibly because we were both in full uniform.

Now, Sergeant Jaget Kumar swans around in his uniform all the time, the better to deter terrorism, pickpockets and people playing their music too loud. But I can normally live without my Metvest. Especially on a Tube train during the morning rush hour in late July when Evian sales are at their peak. The S8 rolling stock is supposed to be air conditioned but, seriously, you wouldn't know it.

Still, it's amazing how even on the most crowded Tube train a police uniform can clear a good ten centimetres of personal space all around your body. The other commuters will literally climb into each other's armpits to avoid touching you. Maybe they think it's bad luck or something.

'Anyway,' said Jaget. 'The thing about these people, right, is that they start learning to track about the same age they can walk. Their dads take them out and teach them, so by the time they're grown up they're experts. They had this young boy and he looked at this trail and he just reeled off all the animals that had gone past in the last couple of days.'

'How did they know he was telling the truth?'

'What?'

'The documentary makers,' I said. 'How did they know he was telling the truth? He could have been making all that shit up.'

'Why would he make it up?'

'Because there's these rich geezers with money and cameras and he figures it's what they want to hear.'

'I believed him, okay?'

I said that I would have set up a low-light camera in a hide overnight and then you could check the boy's account against the video evidence. Jaget said I was missing the point.

'Which was?'

'Maybe the reason Abigail is better at finding ghosts than you,' he said, 'is because that's all you've let her do for the last couple of years. Ten thousand hours and all that.'

'She's been doing more than chasing ghosts,' I said.

'Like what?'

'I don't know,' I said. 'That's what's worrying me.'

Which was when we heard the commotion further

down the carriage. A good solid scream would have been nice, but after two hours of riding the trains at rush hour we'd settle for anything we could get.

'At last,' said Jaget.

Even with our uniforms on, it took us a good five minutes to push our way down the train. And, by the time we reached the spot, everyone was busy trying to pretend nothing had happened.

I made a mental note of the faces in case they became relevant later, before zeroing in on a young white woman in a blue off the peg skirt suit sitting in a seat by the end door. She caught my eye because not only was her face flushed, but she kept sneaking looks at us and then pretending to be madly interested in her Kindle.

Me and Jaget did some professional looming until we'd cleared enough space for me to crouch down and, in my best non-intimidating voice, ask whether she was alright. In case you're wondering, that blokey sing-song timbre with a reassuring touch of regional – in my case cockney – accent is entirely deliberate. We actually practise it in front of a mirror. It's designed to convey the message that we're totally friendly, customer-facing modern police officers who have nothing but your wellbeing at the core of our mission statement . . . but nonetheless we are *not* going to go away until you talk to us. Sorry, but that's just how we roll.

I let Jaget take over, since technically this was his jurisdiction – especially if this turned out to be a common or garden sexual assault. He started by getting her name out of her – Jessica Talacre, aged twenty-four, publicist for a small technical publisher located off Charterhouse Street.

3

'Was that you yelling?' he asked.

'I was just startled,' she said and crossed her arms. 'Someone knocked into me.'

Jaget looked around at the nearby passengers.

'One of these people?'

'It was an accident,' she said. 'They didn't mean to.'

'But it wasn't one of these guys, was it?' I said.

Jessica Talacre looked at me sharply. 'What makes you say that?'

'There was something a bit weird about this person?' I asked.

'What, apart from being a ghost?' she said, and looked defiant and then a bit fearful that we might have the famous white coats stashed about our person.

'What makes you think it was a ghost?' I asked.

'Because,' she said, 'he faded out in front of my eyes.'

I pulled out my notebook and asked if she could give me a description.

'Wait,' she said. 'You *believe* me?'

*

There had been reports suggesting there was a ghost on the Metropolitan Line. Which Jaget brought to me, because disruptive phantasmagoria is the responsibility of the Special Assessment Unit, otherwise known as the Folly, otherwise known as 'those weird bleeders'. Since, despite being an Operational Command Unit, the SAU consisted of me and Detective Chief Inspector Nightingale, and since Inspectors don't get out of bed for anything less than a body in the vicarage, most initial case assessments were done by yours truly.

When I'd first met him, Jaget had been working

for the London Underground division of the British Transport Police but they'd just now re-organised and reassigned him to his very own office at their swanky HQ in Camden Town. Technically he worked directly for the Chief Constable as a trouble shooter and go-to problem solver, but really he was there to deal with the weird shit on the Underground. For this he blamed me.

'You're the one that likes exploring places underground,' I said. 'You walked right into this of your own accord.'

He did admit that it gave him a varied workload. I got to see his brand new office, which would have had a lovely scenic view of the car park and canal if the blinds didn't have to be permanently drawn to prevent people looking in.

'Can't have members of the public seeing what we get up to all day,' said Jaget before passing over a yellow folder full of hardcopy. Normally we shunt files back and forth as email attachments, but the Folly prefers to do things the old-fashioned way. Just in case someone leaks our emails, and also because only one of us currently lives in the twenty-first century.

'I was handed this by Project Guardian,' said Jaget. 'They wanted my advice.'

Project Guardian was a joint BTP/Met/Transport For London/City Police initiative to deal with sexual assaults and offensive behaviour on the transport system. Part of that initiative was improving reporting rates for those offences, which meant convincing victims we were taking them seriously. So when you get a cluster of complaints about assaults by a 'man who wasn't there' you don't just bin them. You pass them to the people who are responsible for weird shit, i.e. me and Jaget.

'A man who wasn't there?' I said.

There had been a cluster of complaints, two men, three women, who either called the Project Guardian hotline or 999 and reported that they had been variously groped, shouted at and, in one case, racially abused.

'All of them on the Metropolitan Line,' said Jaget.

Where it got weird was in the follow ups. When contacted, all five complainants denied the encounter had ever happened and expressed a mixture of surprise and irritation that the police were contacting them. Witnesses and victims changing their mind happens all the time, particularly with hate crimes and domestic abuse, but there was a definite pattern here – so I was wondering if they'd been intimidated.

'Did they follow up the follow up?' I asked.

'They were particularly worried about Amirah Khalil, because of the racial aspect,' said Jaget and showed me the transcript of her initial 999 call – the relevant bits had been highlighted.

CALLER: He called me a dirty Saracen and he was acting totally manic. I'm terrified he's [unintelligible] come back. He scared me there was something . . . [CALL TERMINATED AT SOURCE]

'We think she went into the tunnels north of Baker Street at that point,' said Jaget. 'She didn't call back.'

But Operation Guardian knew her name because she'd called on her mobile, so it was a relatively simple act to trace her to her home address in Watford. There she denied that any such incident had taken place or that she'd called the police.

'I spoke to the officers who interviewed her and they

say they thought she genuinely had no memory of making the call,' said Jaget.

I looked at the picture of Amirah Khalil, a round face, dark eyes. Her family were from Egypt, but she was light enough to pass for Italian or Spanish. Saracen . . . it was an odd insult.

'Was she wearing a head scarf or hijab on the train?'

'You noticed the Saracen thing, right?' said Jaget. 'She was wearing a hijab when they interviewed her – hence the interest.'

Operation Guardian followed up with a second complainant. One Jonathan Pickering of Grove Avenue, Pinner. Mr Pickering had actually been interviewed shortly after he'd made his call. This had been undertaken by a pair of BTP officers who met him, at his own request, at Finchley Road Station within ten minutes of his initial call. According to the BTP officers' statements Mr Pickering had seemed vague and uncertain as to why he'd got off at Finchley Road – when they attempted to take a statement he denied that any incident had taken place. When challenged, they had a logged call from his number after all, Mr Pickering said he had no memory of making a 999 call and expressed surprise and disbelief when the call log of his own phone confirmed that he had.

I checked the transcript of the 999 call. Mr Pickering clearly states that he'd been harassed by 'some weird guy' who called him a 'tinker' and demanded that he 'stand up straight'. There's a pause listed as being two seconds long and then Mr Pickering can be heard asking other passengers 'You saw that right? You saw that? . . . How can you not have fucking seen that?'

Mr Pickering was a coder for a software development company based near the Old Street roundabout, so unlike Ms Khan he would have changed at King's Cross. So no point of correspondence there.

'What do you think?' asked Jaget.

I told him that he'd pretty much had me at 'Saracen' and that I'd take the files home, do a preliminary Falcon assessment, and get back to him the next day.

'Preliminary Falcon assessment?' said Jaget.

'We at the Folly have embraced the potentialities of modern policing,' I said.

*

Our filing system was strictly Edwardian, with our ghost-related material scattered through two different libraries, seemingly randomly archived reports by wizards and county practitioners going back two centuries, and a card file system that was suspiciously incomplete – I suspect whoever was organising it gave up in disgust halfway through.

Fortunately, I also had access to that most modern of office accoutrements: the unpaid teenaged intern in the form of my cousin Abigail Kumara. Who, because it was the summer holidays, had to be kept out of mischief.

'What kind of ghost?' she asked.

'We don't know it's a ghost,' I said. 'Don't make assumptions.'

She rolled her eyes to indicate that only one of us was making assumptions, and it wasn't her. She had a narrow face which could fall into an expression of belligerent suspicion of such power that her teachers said they could feel it even when they were hiding in the staff room. It was her stubbornness, coupled with this expression – and routine everyday low grade racism – that kept her constantly on the verge of a school suspension.

'She's disruptive,' one of her teachers told me, but floundered when I asked her precisely how this disruption manifested itself.

'I don't know,' wailed the teacher. 'She just sits and stares at you and the lesson plan goes out of the window.'

My boss Nightingale, who teaches her Latin, has no such problems.

'If only all my students were so diligent,' he said, which given that I was his only other student was a bit unfair. Abigail didn't have to work a full case load or learn magic. Although I figured the magic wasn't far off.

'You must have known that she would inevitably have to be taught,' said Nightingale.

'I was hoping to wait until she was at least eighteen,' I said, although actually I'd been hoping she'd lose interest . . . but what can you do? A promise is a promise, or as Nightingale put it, 'Either your word is good or it's worthless.'

And magic is difficult, complicated, and carries serious risks. But trying to teach yourself it is almost inevitably fatal. And I reckoned that, left to her own devices, Abigail would have a go at trying to teach herself. So at some point we were going to have to sit down with her parents and explain that we wanted to teach their daughter magic.

'Is it safe?' they'd ask.

'No, it's hideously dangerous, but if we don't teach her she'll probably accidentally kill herself before she's sixteen.'

There's a conversation I was looking forward to.

So a good, thorough, and probably pointless search of the archives was just the thing to stave off that awful day. While Abigail went through the card file I pinned a map of North West London onto the wall in the upstairs reading room and marked out the route of the Metropolitan Line and the locations mentioned in the reports.

The Metropolitan Line runs from the heart of the city at Aldgate out to the northwest beyond the M25, until it peters out just short of the Chilterns. The original plan was to build a railway that ran from the Midlands to Paris with a stop off in London for shopping. That it ended up creating a quarter of modern London instead was a completely unintended consequence, but then the history of my city has always been a series of unintended consequences – just ask Boudicca.

The line emerges into the daylight at Baker Street, leapfrogs the Jubilee Line to reach Wembley Park in just two stops, crosses the North Circular and makes a mad dash for the green belt, only pausing to split in two to spawn a series of commuter suburbs that provide the disaffected middle class youth of London with somewhere to rebel against. Then comes Rickmansworth and disaster – the last vestiges of London are left behind and the line vanishes into the green tinted mists of Buckinghamshire.

Don't get me wrong, I like the countryside. In fact, some of my best friends are geographical features. It's just a tricky place to operate in. Fortunately for me, all seven incidents in Jaget's file took place between Baker Street and Wembley Park. And it was definitely something supernatural. I've seen that fading memory phenomenon before.

Dr Walid has speculated that people under a certain kind of influence might be generating different sets of neurotransmitters, not unlike the ones it's speculated we generate during sleep. In both cases, short term memories are not consolidated into long term memory. In exactly the way our dreams aren't, which is why we forget them. I gave him a call and his best suggestion was that if I could get to a witness early enough they might retain more memories.

'If it is like dream retention,' he said, 'their recounting the events might help them transfer to long term memory.'

He would have liked blood samples as well, but we've found that people are strangely reluctant to give up their bodily fluids to the police in the name of science.

I went through the reports again in the vain hope that something new would jump out before heading downstairs for tea in the atrium. Molly had made something that might have been banana cake, except it had sultanas in it. She was experimenting again – we suspected the influence of *The Great British Bake Off*.

While we had our tea Abigail got out her notebook and started flipping through the pages. I had given her her first notebook a year or so earlier, but this was probably number ten. It was hard to keep track because she refused to let anybody else look at them and, according to her dad, kept them in her room in a lock box that he'd made for her. Her dad's a track maintenance engineer, so when he builds something it's going to be too robust for me to get a sneak peek. Nightingale could probably open it with a wave of his hand, but I didn't need to ask to know he would regard it as an ungentlemanly act.

It was no use pointing out that we were actually policemen, not gentlemen, because Nightingale has a very clear idea where one ends and the other begins. One day, I'm hoping, he'll show me where that line is.

I know Abigail goes out and gets herself into trouble when our backs are turned. I'm pretty certain she was mixed up somehow with a couple of teenaged mispers last summer. And she seems to have picked up some protection from a senior civil servant at the Home Office – although Lady Ty swears blind that it's nothing to do with her.

'On the Metropolitan Line,' said Abigail using her serious voice, 'we have a bunch of public domain hauntings and some verified ghosts, three of which were reported expunged'. The Folly had done a lot less expunging of ghosts than you might expect. In the eighteenth century they were more interested in studying them, and the Victorians were worried they might truly be the souls of human beings so left that sort of thing to the Church. Abigail was of the opinion that if your average vicar had ever truly exorcised a ghost it was only by accident. But there'd been a number of practitioners who were also parsons. Apparently being a country parson was a cushy living up until the late nineteenth century and had involved remarkably little in the way of actual religion.

'There's the ghost of Anne Naylor at Farringdon,' said Abigail. 'Thirteen year old girl murdered in 1758, known as the Screaming Spectre.' There was a pause for some more possibly-not-banana cake. 'Then the famous phantom footprints between Baker Street, St John's Wood and Boudicca's burial site at King's Cross – remember that?'

We'd done it as a field trip – Platform 10 at King's Cross,

which was reputedly the last resting place of the woad-wearing warrior woman. We hadn't found anything, but it had led to a lively discussion about the practicalities of attaching blades to the wheels of your chariot. We got so carried away that a posh middle-aged white woman, no doubt waiting for a train, congratulated me on being an excellent father and for fostering an interest in British history in my daughter.

'Well done you,' she'd said.

There were a couple of verified ghosts of the 'full torso repeating manifestation type' at Finchley Road, but they only manifested when someone fed them some magic. Which we'd done one wet Sunday when Abigail had been particularly restive and I was too lazy to come up with something better.

'I think we should go have a look,' said Abigail.

So I called Jaget and asked him to inform the relevant station control rooms that we'd be out and about that evening. Then we procured a packed supper from Molly and walked up to King's Cross to hop on the Metropolitan Line.

We'd timed it to miss the worst of the rush hour, but it was still packed all the way up to Wembley where we hopped off and waited for a southbound train. We started at the far end of the platform so Abigail had plenty of time to note the train number as it pulled in. The S8 Bombardier rolling stock is a walkthrough train, so there's no fiddling about with doors from carriage to carriage. Being able to see or move down the whole length of the train increases capacity and is a boon to police officers, fare dodgers and pickpockets alike. We walked up its length during the long run back from Wembley Park to Finchley Road feeling for any *vestigia* and trying not to look too much like weirdos.

We got off at Finchley Road, waited for the next train, and repeated the process on the way to Baker Street where we turned around and did it again back up to Wembley. We did the journey a couple more times before stopping off at Finchley to eat our suppers.

Which turned out to be steak and kidney pasties, still warm, with a recycled jam jar full of pickled onions staring out at us like so many eyeballs. We ate the pasties but we both figured that eating the pickles in a public place would constitute a nuisance under the Anti-Social Behaviour, Crime and Policing Act 2014.

There had been a ton of *vestigia* on the trains, but it had all been the routine noise that we'd taken to calling 'engineering background' – random sensations involving bits of metal banging together, the smell of oil and sweat and steam, chips and vinegar, topless pin ups and rolling tobacco.

Nothing that said 'agitated spirit' to either of us.

We were considering whether to do another couple of runs or not when a voice called my name.

A short black man in a blue London Underground shirt was striding down the platform towards us. He was built like a brick shithouse, with broad shoulders and short muscular legs – he also walked with the familiar bantam strut, and that's what I recognised before his face, which had acquired a pair of Malcom X specs and a conservative fade cut that couldn't disguise his receding hairline. His name was Dwain Fletcher and he may have looked older than me, but we'd been in the same year at school. We hadn't been friends exactly, but we'd got along and the last time I'd seen him he was disappearing under a pile of police outside the Camden Palace. We'd been fifteen, and I'd heard later that he'd ended up in a young offenders' institution or emigrated to Canada, or something equally dire.

I stood up and he hugged me briefly.

'Bruv,' he said. 'Remember me?'

I said I did but that I'd heard he'd 'gone away', which I felt covered all the bases.

'Nah, man,' he said. 'I'm respectable.'

He was in fact a station manager for London Underground, currently covering a colleague on maternity leave at Finchley Road. He'd heard that I'd be on his stretch, so he'd kept an eye on the CCTV.

I asked him what he'd been up to, because I didn't want to have to run a PNC check to find out. He'd managed to avoid a spell at Her Majesty's pleasure, but his mum had sent him back to Jamaica in the strange belief this might straighten him out. Which it did, but not for the reason his mum thought.

'They're mad there,' he said. 'So I came back and went to college.'

And got a job with the Underground and a wife and two kids and a semi in Redbridge. He got out his phone and showed me pictures. His wife was mixed race and had a serious face. The children were six and four years old and looked like trouble, but in a good way.

I told him they seemed brilliant while Abigail made gagging motions behind his back.

He asked if we were really ghost hunting, and I said we were.

'What, like officially?'

'Officially secret,' I said because discretion is supposed to be, if not our middle name, at least a nickname we occasionally answer to when we remember.

'You want to be looking further up,' he said. 'At Pinner. That's where all the ghostly stuff is.'

'Who says?'

'You know,' he said. 'Track walkers, engineers, superstitious folk.'

I expressed polite scepticism, but Dwain insisted that it was true. I said we'd look into it, and we exchanged numbers and promises to come round for supper and meet the missus before me and Abigail hopped on the next train back to King's Cross.

As we travelled Abigail consulted her notebooks.

'There's got to be a better way to check the trains,' she said.

'It would probably be easier if we waited for them to all park up,' I said. 'You know – like in a depot or something.'

2

The Neasden Postboy

At peak capacity the Metropolitan Line runs twenty-two trains per hour, and at the end of the day those units – because that's the technical term – have to be stored somewhere. That's fifty-eight trains, each one about one hundred and twenty metres long,[1] so the depots have to be a bit on the largish side. You catch a glimpse of this enormity as you swish past on your way to Wembley Park, but you don't appreciate the sheer fuck-off size of the place until you walk in and see a couple of thousand tons of rolling stock laid out in ranks in the marshalling yard.

'That's a lot of trains,' I said.

The depot management weren't happy about us being there, and only agreed to let us in because we had Jaget with us and agreed to wear hard hats and reflective jackets and not wander off unaccompanied. It took a bit of fast talking on Nightingale's part to explain that we needed a bit of privacy to work properly. It ended up being a messy compromise and it didn't help that Jaget hadn't wanted to come out and play in the first place.

---

[1] Note for Reynolds: that's a bit over the length of an American football pitch. Sorry, field.

'It's fish and chip night tonight,' he said, and scowled.

Fish and chip night was a Kumar family tradition that dated back to when Jaget was courting his wife and they used to meet in the last white English-owned fish and chip shop in Wembley on the basis that none of their relatives would go in there.

'It was proper fish and chips too,' Jaget had said, although they'd had to smuggle in a few condiments to take the edge off the blandness. 'They closed down years ago – it's a Pret now I think.'

I'd asked why their relatives might have objected to them going out. Jaget said it wasn't like that at all. 'Our families were seriously intertwined at the Aunty level, and when they found out they practically died of happiness. We just wanted a bit of time and privacy before our families steamrollered us into the temple.'

So every month they palmed off the kids onto their – still presumably ecstatic – families, cooked fish and chips and spent the rest of the evening in. Mrs Kumar was not going to be happy.

'Now you've made me hungry,' said Abigail, whose parents had become remarkably relaxed about her late night ghost-hunting jaunts.

'We'll grab an Ethiopian on the way over,' I said.

But we got Kurdish instead and finished it off while waiting for all the stock to arrive.

The Underground works all day and all evening, which means the brave men and women in high-visibility orange who keep it running have to work all night. The depot is so full of people banging bits of metal together and scraping things to make sparks that if you squinted you'd swear they were about to launch a last desperate attack against the Death Star.

Fortunately Abigail had a list of trains that had been running in the relevant area and a sombre looking engineer called Hiran to point us in the right direction. In proper Scooby Gang fashion we split up, with me and Jaget taking one side of the depot while Nightingale and Abigail took the other. We got the third rail safety lecture first, even though the sidings we'd be checking were powered down.

'Always assume the power is on,' Jaget said. 'Because you don't want to find out the hard way.'

And since the power was off we had to climb in through the driver's emergency access door at the front of the train. Hiran warned us again to be on our best behaviour and went off, sensibly, to keep an eye on Abigail.

With only the amber yard lights filtering through the windows on one side and no power it was amazingly dark and still. Tube trains are like clubs – they're well creepy with no people and without the hum of the motors and air conditioning.

'What are we looking for anyway?' asked Jaget.

'Just see if you can feel anything strange,' I said.

'Like what?'

'Like something that doesn't belong,' I said. 'But isn't your imagination.'

'How do you tell the difference?'

'Practice,' I said.

Not that we got any practice on that train.

We went back to the front where, as we had been strictly instructed, we waited for Hiran to come back and escort us to the next train along.

Which was darker, stiller and emptier.

It wasn't until the fifth train that we found something. Three carriages down Jaget pointed at one of the transverse seats near the end and said, 'There.'

'What?'

'Don't know,' he said. 'Something.'

And it *was* something. I knew that once I got within half a metre. The smell of horse sweat and the sound of distant shouting. I told Jaget he was right and he nodded sagely.

'I'm getting the hang of this, aren't I?' he said.

I told him he was, but asked him not to ever do anything magical without checking with me first. I called Nightingale and told him I was going to do some magic and asked him to see if he could watch for a wider reaction. Then we switched our phones and airwaves off and I conjured up a werelight.

I opened my palm and let the light hover. Jaget had assured me that all the power systems on the train were off so there was no chance of my wrecking five million quid's worth of rolling stock.

Normally when you feed a ghost it appears all in one mass, taking on the illusion of solidity as it noms up the magic. This one was like a glitch in a computer game, its torso bent over backwards at the waist, legs pumping spasmodically, arms outstretched, head held vertically on the end of an obscenely elongated neck. Despite the contortion, we could see that he was a young man dressed in a red eighteenth century riding jacket and knee breeches. His mouth moved and formed words but they were hard to catch, like when someone is trying to talk over loud music in a club.

'Where is the postmaster?' he said.

I checked my werelight, which was burning yellow. This was odd, because they usually turn red as the ghost sucks up the power.

'I have a letter,' he said, the voice wavering in and out. 'An urgent letter.'

His head twisted on the neck, so that it faced us, and both me and Jaget unconsciously bent sideways to keep it right way up.

'But I can't find the postmaster,' he said. 'And I have a letter.'

'Who is the letter from?' I asked.

'It's from the palace. Where is the postmaster? Where is the magistrate? I have a letter for the magistrate.'

'Give me the letter,' I said. 'I can deliver it to the magistrate.'

The ghost frowned and for the first time his eyes focused on us.

'Are you his servants?' he asked.

'Yes,' I said. 'You can trust us.'

The ghost's right arm twitched in our direction as if he was trying to reach for us, but couldn't get control of his limbs. His eyes closed in resignation.

'Alas,' said the ghost. 'I have run my course.' And with that his head fell off, just dropped off his shoulders and straight through the floor of the carriage. And, before we could react to that, his arms and legs separated from his torso and fell away. For a moment his torso hung on its own and I could see the chest moving as if he was still breathing, before it too dropped out of sight.

'Okay,' said Jaget after a pause. 'That's the second most freakiest thing you've ever shown me.'

I snapped off the werelight.

'That was really odd,' I said.

'Yeah, even by your standards of odd that was odd,' said Jaget. 'What next?'

I opened my notebook. 'We record it,' I said. 'And then we move on.'

That's one of the golden rules of police work – just because you've found one body doesn't mean there isn't a second a couple of metres further on. Finish whatever search you started if only so you don't have to come back and do it all again later.

I turned my phone back on and told the engineer that we were ready to board the next train, which turned out to be a bust, as did the next two. In the fourth I felt not one but two separate hot spots at opposite ends of the train. I gave both the werelight treatment, but neither responded. We dutifully made a note of the carriage and moved on.

In our whole line of trains I only found one more ghost – that of a plump white woman in a low-cut Jane Austen dress. Even with me pumping up the werelight she remained so transparent I couldn't tell you what colour the dress was. She appeared aware of us and her mouth moved, but there was no sound. She only lasted thirty seconds before, scowling and with her fists bunched in frustration, she shattered, falling to pieces as if she'd been made of porcelain.

Once we'd written her up and checked the last of our trains I turned on my mobile and called Nightingale. It went straight to voicemail, so we jumped down and Hiran walked us across the yard towards the side Nightingale and Abigail were supposed to be working.

We found Nightingale under a raised floodlight by the hangar-sized maintenance building, jotting down notes.

'Where's Abigail?' I asked.

Nightingale pointed down the side of the building.

'She popped off down there,' he said.

'To do what?' I asked. Nightingale is often aghast – his word – at the restrictions we put on young people and he feels modern adults are far too overprotective. But even given that background, he still had way more faith in Abigail's common sense than I did.

'She's up to something clandestine, I'm sure,' he said.

I left Jaget with Nightingale and stalked off to see what Abigail had got into now. There was a raised platform running the length of the workshop. Hiran had told us that we were fine as long as we stayed on these and I hoped Abigail hadn't wandered off.

I walked the length of the platform, and as I reached the end I heard Abigail speaking.

'I can't talk now,' she said and I guessed she was tucked out of sight at the front of the train.

I heard another voice, high pitched, breathy but too quiet for me to make out the words. Nosiness is practically a professional requirement in the police, so I had no qualms about quietly easing myself closer so I could eavesdrop.

'Because Peter is here,' said Abigail, then a pause. 'You're the ones that don't want him to know.'

The other speaker either laughed or had a coughing fit.

'I should tape you and sell it to *Fox Watch*,' said Abigail.

'There's a house,' said a different voice, with the same breathy texture, only crisper and better enunciated. 'It sits out on a hill at the end of the line. It used to stand alone but now it's crowded round – there are stories and ghosts.'

'Stories?'

I could hear the shrug in the voice.

'Stories,' it said.

The rougher voice said something.

'The kind of stories that have power,' said the softer voice.

A low snarl.

'He's here,' said the softer voice. 'Laters.'

I counted to ten and walked around the front of the train. Abigail was standing looking out over the tangles of metal rails and power junctions that stretched away to the edge of the depot. She had her headphones in and was nodding her head as if listening to music – a nice touch, that, I thought.

'Who were you talking to?' I asked.

She made a show of registering my presence and pulling one earpiece out before asking me 'What?'

'Who were you talking to just now?'

'Nobody,' she said. 'Are we finished?'

'We are,' I said. 'But for you the work has just begun.'

*

All right, we took her home to sleep first. But I picked her up nice and early the next morning and introduced her to the control room at Finchley Road where, with Dwain's help, she was going to match up the carriage numbers we'd gathered with CCTV footage. Starting with the carriage where Jaget had found our eighteenth century postboy.

These used to run the post up and down the treacherous roads of Britain between the major cities, pausing only to change horses and rifle through the contents of their bags. It was a lot like the Pony Express, except without the glamour, with more rain and added highwaymen. This explained why our ghost was carrying an urgent letter and looking for 'the postmaster'. But the question was whether he'd been what me and Abigail had taken to calling an entity, a simulacrum or a looper. There are various old terms, some in Latin, for the various types of ghost but since none of them are consistent with each other we decided to make our own jargon up. Saved time all round.

The first factor is *intensity* on a scale of one to ten *annies* – where one annie is that strange sensation that somebody is standing looking over your shoulder and ten annies, very rare, being when you only realise someone's a ghost because they walk through a wall. You can boost a ghost's intensity by feeding it magic and we're pretty certain that most ghosts are powered by the accumulated *vestigia* in their environment. Of all the natural materials, stone retains *vestigia* the best, which is why all old houses tend to be haunted.

The second factor is *volition*, which is broken down into three categories. *Loopers* are the most common type of ghost. They're basically recordings where the ghost repeats a series of actions, painting the wall of a train tunnel, screaming for their lost baby, boarding a nonexistent tram in Aldwych. The longest loop we've found in the records lasted sixty-seven hours, and the shortest seven seconds.

Entities are the other end of the spectrum. These are ghosts that talk and react as if they're alive. You can have a conversation with them and they appear to display comprehension and even some theory of mind. Me and Abigail have arguments about whether this constitutes them being 'alive' – I haven't met one yet that I thought would pass the Turing Test. The literature is split between whether they are the souls of the departed trapped in the material plane or impressions left behind by the dead.

Simulacra are the ghosts that lie between *entities* and *loopers*. To me and Abigail they appear like characters in a computer game. However skilfully programmed they are, their actions and speech quickly become repetitive and stereotyped.

Intensity and volition appear to be unrelated, so that some daylight visible ghosts merely repeat themselves while you only find some of the chatty ones by accident, they are so faint in their presence. One very late Oxford professor scared me to death by popping into existence while I was casting a werelight in the tunnels under Kew Garden. One day, when they finally let me back in the place, I'll see if I can find her again.

These things run on a spectrum, of course, so the terminology can break down at the boundaries. But we'd tentatively identified the postboy as a five annie simulacrum. Mind you, I've never seen a ghost come apart the way the postboy had the night before.

'It was like it was disintegrating,' I told Nightingale

over breakfast. 'Literally losing cohesion in front of our eyes.'

'Are you sure it was a ghost?' asked Nightingale.

I'd had to think about that. There are other incorporeal things out there, rare but very real. Some of them eat ghosts and others can get into your head and twist your life out of shape.

'It felt like a ghost,' I said. 'It had that air of sadness you always feel around them.'

Nightingale smiled at me over his coffee cup. 'An aura of melancholy hardly constitutes empirical evidence what would our Doctors Walid and Vaughan say?'

Still, disassembling ghosts would have to wait because while Abigail was wading through CCTV I was cramming for my National Investigators Exam and committing to memory the many steps needed to ensure health and safety at a crime scene. That's the health and safety of the police and associated law enforcement professionals. Obviously when you're securing a murder scene you don't have to worry about HSE complaints from the victim.

Fortunately, when you grow up in a flat as small as my parents' you learn how to do your homework in cafés and libraries.

I was just wrestling with what exactly were the legal powers available to the police when securing a crime scene, and the vital question of whether or not to have another round of toast, when Abigail texted me that she had something to show me.

Not only had she found all the relevant footage, she'd edited out the boring bits, spliced it all together, added musical backing in the shape of Ella Henderson's 'Ghost' and transferred it to her laptop so we could watch it without interfering in the smooth operation of Dwain's control room.

I was fairly certain the CCTV footage was proprietary, so I checked with Dwain who said he didn't even know it was possible to transfer it out like that.

'You're not going to report us, right?' I asked.

'You're kidding,' he said. 'I've just hired her to optimise my home entertainment system.'

I asked Abigail how much she was planning to charge.

'Client confidentiality,' she said. 'But if you want your stuff at the coach house fixed I can give you a quote.'

*

We popped out of the station and round the corner to a dubious fried chicken stroke internet café where we could look dodgy and technological without drawing adverse attention. Abigail handed me a USB pen and I transferred the file over to my laptop where it nearly broke my player.

'You want to get that upgraded,' said Abigail.

The video started with a brief title sequence before opening on an interior shot of an S8 carriage, shot from the high, wide angle point of view of a ceiling mounted CCTV camera.

'This is the unit where you found the postboy,' said Abigail.

Titles crashed in with the opening chords of the song, starkly white against black – POSTBOY – and below that the unit serial number and a time stamp. Then the actual CCTV footage faded up to reveal a familiarly rammed carriage wall to wall with commuters and, judging by the light, running above ground in daylight.

'Top left hand corner,' said Abigail.

I saw it – a flicker of movement.

'Can you . . .' I started, but Abigail told me to wait.

The sequence repeated, only now in grainy close up.

'Sorry about the quality,' she said. 'I didn't have any clean-up tools.'

We didn't need them, because even with the blur and grain it was easy to see the ripple amongst the passengers as they reacted to a patch of empty space. You didn't need much of an imagination to insert the figure of postboy working his way up the carriage.

'Why can't we see him?'

'You're asking me?' said Abigail.

'We have photographs back at the Folly,' I said. 'You can see the ghosts on those.'

Abigail said she was dubious about the collection of faded sepia prints we'd unearthed in the mundane library. She'd done her own experiments both with her phone and a vintage Leica camera she'd found inside one of the storage cupboards in the Folly lecture theatre.

'What were you even doing in there?' I asked.

'Having a look around,' she said.

'How did you get them developed?'

'There's a darkroom in the metal working lab.'

And she'd taught herself photographic developing off the internet. Because of course she had.

Her theory was that the visible aspect of the ghosts,

the bit that reflected photons which could register on our eyeballs or London Underground's CCTV, was very tenuous. Since they were manifesting in full daylight they were lost in the contrast.

But people had reported seeing them even if the memories had quickly faded.

'Maybe human eyesight is still better than the cameras?'

I ran the sequence back and forth, watching the passengers reacting to a presence that wasn't visible on screen.

'*Vestigia*,' I said. 'Our brains get additional information from non-corporeal aspects of the ghost and automatically use that to fill in the gaps in the visual information.' Human visual perception being more like educated guesswork than a camera recording.

'Nice,' said Abigail. 'Very plausible.'

'Yeah, but just because it's plausible doesn't mean it's true.'

'Testable?' asked Abigail.

'You've been reading books again, haven't you?'

Abigail rocked the footage back and forth.

'Testable?' she asked again.

'I don't know,' I said. 'You tell me.' And, before she could open her mouth to speak, 'But not today. What else did you find?'

Abigail ran her little fan film forward to reveal a number of other incidents including Jonathan Pickering and Amirah Khalil's close encounters.

'One incident every weekday for the last nine weekdays, most of them in the stretch between Wembley Park and Harrow on the Hill, and none closer in than

Finchley Road. All of them travelling into London during the morning rush hour.'

'Ghost commuter,' I said. 'At least now we've narrowed down where to look.'

3

The French Lieutenant's Commuter

It's hard to conduct an interview on a rush hour train, and normally we'd have gone somewhere quieter with hot and cold running coffee, but we didn't know how long the woman's memories would last. I didn't even dare wait until we could bail at the next station. So Jaget used his uniformed presence to create a perimeter while I evicted a young white man with a shovel beard off an adjacent seat and sat down next to her.

Likewise, you usually take down a few details to calm the witness down and reinforce the notion that you are an authority figure before taking a statement. But this time I just settled for her name: Jessica Talacre.

'I thought he was French to start with,' said Jessica. 'He sounded French, at least I think it was French. He was shouting at me and he seemed angry.'

I asked if she could remember what the man had looked like, black or white or . . .

'Mixed,' said Jessica. 'But lighter than you, with curly hair in those things.' She raised her index finger to her scalp and made circular motions.

'Ringlets?' I asked.

'Yeah,' she said. 'That and his teeth were bad.'

He was also wearing a long old-fashioned 'Mr Darcy'

coat in heavy material but not, unfortunately, in red. So not a match with our Neasden Depot ghost. Jessica seemed startled when I asked for details of his trousers but remembered enough to confirm that the ghost had been wearing breeches and white stockings – she hadn't seen his shoes.

I asked her if she could remember what the French had sounded like and she gave me a strange look.

'What French?' she asked.

I kept going, but it was too late. In less than ten minutes from the end of the incident Jessica Talacre had lost all memory of it. I gave her my card and asked her to call me if she remembered additional details, but it was obvious that she thought I was bonkers.

'Want to keep going?' asked Jaget as we wrote up our notes.

'If Abigail's right, then that's our sighting for the morning,' I said.

'And if she isn't?' asked Jaget, because police and scientists have that in common.

'Then hopefully she'll spot it,' I said. Abigail was cheerfully playing Big Brother in Finchley Road's control centre, which just went to show that when it came to London Underground's regulations my friend Dwain hadn't totally reformed.

And, speaking of Abigail . . .

'Let's take a ride up to Amersham,' I said. 'I want to check something out.'

*

Amersham is well out of our manor, being in the County of Buckinghamshire and thus subject to the cool and professional attentions of the TVP, who are never referred to by their colleagues in the Met as the Chav Valley Police. So as we rode the train back up the line I called ahead and let them know we would be poking about, in full uniform, around their patch. They didn't seem bothered, but they did want a firm commitment that we'd warn them before doing anything drastic.

'Like what?' I asked.

Like demolishing any landmarks, said the Thames Valley Police.

'Good one,' said I.

They said they weren't joking, but I'm almost a hundred percent certain they were.

So, off to not-actually-very-historic Amersham we went. There is a medieval core that dates back to the tenth century but the railway station and the modern town sit on a plateau between two rivers – the Misbourne and the Chess. A quick follow up call to Nightingale established that neither were known to possess genius loci.

'Although you should remember, Peter,' he said, 'that not every entity associated with the natural world is as garrulous as Mother Thames's daughters. My mother once told me that the stream at the bottom of our garden had its own fairy guardian and even though I went as far as to construct a hide I never caught so much as a glimpse.'

I wondered if there had really been a fairy guardian or whether his mum had been looking for a way of getting the youngest child of six out from under her feet.

'Incidentally, why on earth are you visiting Amersham?' he asked.

'There's this house,' I said. 'Used to sit all alone on a hill . . .'

Back in 1929 a pair of likely lads made the first of many attempts to drag the English out of their cosy brick hobbit holes and ascend into the future borne aloft on gleaming cubes of white rendered concrete. Thus was High and Over House brought into being upon a hill overlooking the small but rapidly growing town of Amersham. The locals hated it – but I've got to say, if you have to build a monstrous flat roofed modernist pile, then it might as well have decent proportions.

Me and Jaget proceeded out of the train station down through the late Victorian and Edwardian shopping parades and terraces and then left up the hill through lines of faux Edwardian semi-detached houses until he practically stumbled on the entrance. The modernist splendour of High and Over now being largely hidden behind an enormous hedge and old growth trees.

The woman who answered the door gave a familiar little start when she saw us and hesitated before saying, 'Ah. Yes.'

We know that reaction well – it is the cry of the guilty middle class homeowner.

This sort of thing always creates a dilemma since the scale of guilt you're dealing with ranges from using a hosepipe during a ban to having just finished cementing your abusive husband into the patio.

The trick to ascertaining whether it's time to rush in or back away slowly is to say as little as possible while looming and adopting a friendly grin that edges into the menacing. Asking ambiguous but leading questions can also help.

'Good afternoon,' said Jaget. 'Is this your house?'

The women was white, late forties, brown hair cut in a bob, blue eyes, straight nose, pointed chin, narrow mouth, no dimples – it pays to remember these details in case you have to construct an e-fit later. She was wearing prefaded designer jeans and a white blouse with ruffles at the collar and wrists. No obvious dirt stains on her knees or blood stains on the blouse, so if there was a dead husband it had happened long enough ago for her to clean up.

'This house?' asked the woman.

'Yes ma'am,' I said. 'This house.'

She looked over her shoulder as if seeing the interior for the first time.

'Yes, I suppose so,' she said. 'And my husband of course, we own it, yes.'

I know it sounds cruel, but nothing gladdens the heart of the police quite like the sight of a potential customer so off balance that one good nudge will get you a result.

Jaget judged the pause perfectly, giving the woman enough time to almost relax before asking, 'Is there something wrong?'

'I just found them, okay?' she said. 'I buried them because I didn't know what else to do. But it wasn't me who poisoned them.'

'Poisoned who?' asked Jaget.

She told us, and as she did I realised I'd been played good and proper.

'You'd better show us, ma'am,' I said.

The charnel pit was round the back, down a flight of white garden steps, to a sloping lawn and beyond the round swimming pool where the garden proper merged into the woods. I could see where the turfs had been cut and re-laid. The owner provided me with a shovel and I carefully stripped off the turf and the first ten centimetres of soil.

'Damn,' said Jaget. 'It's a fox apocalypse.'

I counted six just on the top layer – I don't know enough about foxes to be sure, but there were at least two smaller specimens that may have been adolescents. None of them seemed large enough to be one of Abigail's talking variety but, like I said, what do I know?

The woman found the first victim floating in her swimming pool a fortnight earlier. She'd assumed that it had fallen in and drowned.

'So I wrapped it in a Waitrose bag,' she said. 'One of those big ones with the handles that you're supposed to buy because it's greener.' She considered whether she could just pop it in amongst the rest of rubbish for collection, but thought she'd read that it might damage the council's incinerator. So she decided to pick out a pleasant spot in the woods to bury it.

'The woods were planted by the original owner,' said the current owner. 'Bernard Ashmole, he was curator of the British Museum.'

'The foxes?' asked Jaget.

'I found the next two while I was carrying the first to its grave,' she said. 'Ironically.'

Then another three along a line from the bottom of the garden to the pool.

'As if they were trying to reach the water,' she said. 'Perhaps whatever killed them made them thirsty or, I don't know, hot, feverish?'

I asked her if she had any idea who might be responsible.

'Oh, one of those lot.' She waved her hand airily at the ranks of dull looking mid-sixties semis that rolled down the hill towards the old town. 'They move out of the city but they want everything to be as nice and tidy and as convenient as living in London.'

Jaget coughed and banged his chest theatrically.

'Sorry,' he said. 'It's all the clean air.'

I asked the woman if she had a tarpaulin or plastic sheeting and, while Jaget helped her fetch it, I called Thames Valley Police. They were happy to know that High and Over House, a Grade II* listed building I might add, was still standing and that the problem was something that the local CID could handle.

While we waited for the local Morse impersonators to turn up, the homeowner served us a rather nice tea on the lawn.

'I'm not in trouble, am I?' she asked.

'Nah,' I said. 'But whoever was poisoning those foxes should seriously consider moving abroad.'

*

We managed to get back to London before the rush hour started and I spent the last part of the afternoon compiling my notes for one of the demonstration investigations I'd have to present to my invigilator as part of the detective's exam.

Meanwhile, Abigail had Latin with Nightingale, which I'm not going to say she enjoys exactly, but I think she gets more satisfaction out of it than I do.

Once we were both done and we'd had late tea I tackled her about the foxes.

'Serves you right for eavesdropping,' said Abigail. 'Don't it?'

The evening had turned warm and muggy and Bedford Way was full of traffic and exhaust fumes. I was running Abigail to her parents' house because it's part of the agreement, but also because I'd promised to pop in and see my mum. My parents live on the same estate as Abigail's so I often combine the chores.

'I wasn't eavesdropping,' I said. 'I was gathering intelligence. And you're supposed to notify me when you talk to weird creatures.'

'But they're not weird, are they?' said Abigail. 'They're just foxes – nothing more London than foxes.'

'Foxes that talk?'

'So, they've got a descended larynx and tongue,' said Abigail. 'Big deal.'

'And bigger brains,' I said.

'That's an assumption,' she said. 'Some other mechanism could be involved.'

'But they only talk to *you*,' I said. 'How come?'

'Maybe if you stopped rushing about and stayed still for five minutes you might spot all the stuff going on around you,' she said.

'And?' I asked, because there's always an 'and' with Abigail.

'I used to buy them kebabs,' she said.

'Kebabs?'

'Well, you can't feed them stockfish, can you?' she said. 'It's too spicy.'

'Obviously.'

'Because they're English foxes, right?'

'So Nando's is fine?'

'Don't be stupid,' said Abigail. 'I can't afford Nando's.'

I was going to ask Abigail whether the foxes preferred their takeaway delivered or à la rubbish bin, but then I found myself thinking of Nightingale's fairy spotting hide and decided that maybe Abigail was right. Maybe it was time to slow down and see if I couldn't lure my railways ghosts to me.

Only I figured I was going to need something a bit more mystical than a kebab.

So, when I got back from my parents' I hunted out Nightingale who was shining his shoes in the kitchen. Molly had spread newspapers across the big oak farmhouse table and, I estimated, about a quarter of all Nightingale's good shoes were arrayed along it like an exhibit from the Victoria and Albert Museum – men's footwear; a history.

Nightingale was sitting at the end of the table dressed in a white dress shirt with silver and black sleeve garters and an Edwardian butler's apron, attacking a wicked pair of Barker Alderney's, which I supposed were there to represent the early 21st century.

Molly was in a seat beside him, polishing a parallel line of silverware. With her in her maid's outfit, the pair of them looked like something from a Japanese manga – presumably they kept their weapons hidden under the table.

'I met a chap in India,' said Nightingale as he buffed up the toes, 'who told me that a wise man takes time to pay attention to the things he uses in his everyday life.

He believed that even inanimate objects had souls that responded to nurturing.'

'Was he a practitioner?' I asked.

'Good Lord no,' said Nightingale. 'A street typist in Calcutta. He made a living typing legal documents and letters for people who didn't own their own typewriter. The occasional love poem, too, I believe.'

He paused to examine the finish on the shoes and, satisfied he could use them as an emergency shaving mirror, replaced them on the table and picked up the next pair.

'The natives held a festival every year where they venerated their tools,' said Nightingale. His friend, he never did learn his proper name, would carefully clean his British Empire Model 12, daub it with turmeric paste, bedeck it with flowers and, on the day of the festival, worship it as if it were a household idol.

'And the moral of this story is?' I asked.

'I don't think there is one,' said Nightingale. 'Except that one should always look after one's kit.'

'Is there a way to attract ghosts?' I asked.

'In what sense?' asked Nightingale.

I explained about our evidence that at least one ghost per day was riding down the Metropolitan Line each morning and then disintegrating messily. He'd never heard of ghosts 'dying' in quite that fashion before.

'Odd,' he said. 'Do you think their condition grew worse as a function of time or distance?'

'Impossible to tell,' I said, mentally giving him full marks for use of the word 'function'. 'Since they've all been travelling, it could be both.'

'So we'd really want to intercept them as early as

possible.' Nightingale put down his brush and used a white linen cloth to clean excess polish off the edges of the soles. 'Harrow on the Hill is the last stop before the line divides. Since we don't know which branch they're coming down, I suggest we establish our lure there.'

'So you *can* lure ghosts,' I said.

'You have yourself,' said Nightingale. 'The ritual you used to summon Wallpenny in Covent Garden, remember?'

'I remember almost getting sucked into a pit,' I said. 'And then bouncing off a tree.'

'That was a particularly difficult situation, and an oversight on my part,' said Nightingale. 'I misapprehended the nature of the threat. What we shall do tomorrow is literally child's play.'

'You've done this before?'

'Back at my old school,' he said. 'During the summer term when it was light in the evenings.'

The younger boys would sneak off the grounds and into the adjacent woods, build a campfire and see what they could attract in the way of the local supernatural.

'And swap comics and tuck of course,' he said. 'Everybody did it, and the masters must have been aware. There could be as many as five campfires going in the woods on some nights.'

Each one a group of boys from a different year. As they got older, the focus used to change – with the older boys drinking and smoking and occasionally playing pranks on the younger.

'Did it work?' I asked.

'Oh, undoubtedly,' said Nightingale. 'Ballantine junior and I once managed to induce the whole of 3B to wet themselves by pretending to be werewolves. Matron was not pleased, and I was caned by the headmaster personally.' Which apparently was a great honour because the headmaster was known to have progressive views and to be against caning in principle. Although obviously not in practice.

'I meant in attracting the supernatural,' I said.

Nightingale shook his hand from side to side.

'Mixed results there, I'm afraid,' he said. 'I'm sure Spotty was hoping for a wood nymph. And there were always rumours of giant spiders and centaurs. I would have liked to have met a centaur, still . . .' he caught my expression and quickly added, 'But any number of ghosts. They must have been the best fed spirits in the whole of England.'

'You didn't start this tradition, right?'

'Lord no,' said Nightingale. 'Squirts had been out in the woods since the school was founded, and they were still at it in 1939.'

When I had a spare moment there was definitely going to have to be a field trip with Toby and my surveying gear to what I suspected was the most magic-saturated spot in England.

'So: bright and early tomorrow morning,' said Nightingale. 'Might be an idea to bring a thermos. Do you think Sergeant Kumar can get us in there before the trains start?'

I said it would be no problem.

Nightingale glanced over to where Toby the wonder dog was asleep in his basket.

'When was your last set of detection experiments?'

'Last month.' It had been proving increasingly hard

43

to persuade Toby to take part in any magic detecting. I'd been trying to teach myself to use a spectrograph I'd discovered while cleaning up the lab.

Nightingale grinned.

'In that case,' he said, 'it might be time to unleash the hounds.'

4

The Harrow Schoolgirl

O r precisely 'the hound' singular, or even more precisely 'the yappy little terrier'. Who incidentally was as happy at being turfed out of his basket at four in the morning as I was. Me and Nightingale decided to leave Abigail to her beauty sleep and we picked Jaget up on our way through Wembley.

The railway hit Harrow on the Hill in 1880 and it's been downhill ever since, culminating in one of those formless red brick shopping centres which artfully combines a complete lack of aesthetic quality with a total disregard for the utilitarian function for which it is built. As a result, your average shopper has only to spend ten minutes inside to be reduced to a state of quiet desperation. Primark has the right idea, being right by the entrance so that fleeing punters would grab the closest approximation to whatever it was they wanted before running screaming into the night.

I'm told that the rest of Harrow, apart from the posh bit on top of the hill, is your bog-standard leafy London outer suburb – if that's what floats your boat. Jaget says that there's some good Tamil restaurants, but we never got to find out because we never got further than the WHSmith's across the road that day.

The station itself had been rebuilt in the 1920s with art deco waiting rooms with rounded ends like the gondolas on an airship. We set up at the south end of the station, which wasn't ideal because coming in from the north there was a chance that any ghost passenger might only spot us on the way out. But we didn't have any choice because the station control room and consequent electronics were at the north end by the transfer bridge and exits. After a couple of years of experiments I was pretty confident I could estimate where the area of magical effect was going to be, but it's best not to take risks with major infrastructure assets.

Especially when the owners haven't totally forgiven you for what happened at Oxford Circus, which was totally . . . never mind.

We arrived in pre-dawn before the first train. The maintenance engineers were coming off tracks in the half light – a mass of high visibility jackets and tired faces. 'Mr Nightingale sir,' called a voice and Mr Kamara, Abigail's father, stepped out from the crowd and approached us.

'Good morning, Mr Kamara,' said Nightingale as they shook hands. 'I didn't know you were working this stretch.'

Mr Kamara was a short wiry man who had, according to my mum, been a dangerous midfielder in the terrifying Maradona[2] mould back in Sierra Leone. The son

---

[2] Note for Reynolds: Diego Maradona was a short arse Argentinian soccer player who, despite not being averse to a bit of handball, was awe inspiring in his ability to race up the length of the pitch, bypassing opposing players as if they weren't there, and then slamming the ball into the back of the net.

of one of my Mum's father's other wives, he'd grown up poor and uneducated. He'd have probably spent the rest of his life as a subsistence farmer if the RUF hadn't overrun his village and killed or mutilated most of his immediate family. According to family legend he taught himself to read from discarded newspapers while a refugee in Freetown before being brought to London by sympathetic relatives. Once here he caught up on six years of missing schooling, got an apprenticeship and became a railway maintenance engineer.

This probably explained why he enthusiastically embraced Abigail's extracurricular studies at the Folly – especially when he learnt that she'd be taking extra GCSEs out of school . . . even if they were Latin and Greek.

'And it gets me out of the flat, don't it,' Abigail had said. And when I asked her whether her dad worried she'd take a degree in Classics rather than one of the African holy trinity of medicine, law or engineering, she told me, 'Dad doesn't know what Classics is, you know – he still has trouble with some of the big words. I have to help him fill in forms.'

He needn't have worried anyway. Abigail was on course to get straight A-stars in maths, physics and chemistry. My old chemistry teacher, who was still teaching at the school, must have been well pleased.

'We go where we're needed, don't we?' said Mr Kamara to Nightingale. 'Just like policemen.' He turned to me and asked what we were up to. Strangely enough, I didn't say we were going to try and attract a ghost off a passing Tube train. I told him we were responding to reports of suspicious activity.

'You mean devils?' he asked. Devils being the Sierra Leonean term for anything spiritual and morally ambiguous.

'Not devils,' I said. 'Ghosts.'

He gave me a grim smile.

'Why would you want to talk to ghosts?'

'We don't want to talk to them per se,' said Nightingale. 'It's just that we'd like to ask them a few questions.'

'What can the dead say?' said Mr Kamara. 'Besides that they don't like being dead.'

Nightingale indicated this was what we were here to find out. Before Abigail's dad headed home I asked if I could borrow his orange high-viz waistcoat.

'I'll drop in on my way back,' I said.

I tied Toby's lead to a convenient lamppost just by where we planned to set up. He yawned, looked around at the grey dawn and give a resigned sigh before curling up and going back to sleep.

Nightingale looked up the platform to where Mr Kamara was striding up the stairs. 'You understand that when the time comes to teach Abigail the forms and wisdoms we will, perforce, have to gain permission from her parents.'

'That's something to look forward to,' I said. 'Do we have to?'

'What do you think?'

I *thought* she was talking to unidentified fox-things behind our back, and that she'd definitely been out having adventures of her own last summer. Once you know something is possible, it's so much easier to work out how it is done.

'I was hoping to wait until she was old enough to vote,' I said.

'Genius runs on its own schedule,' said Nightingale.

I didn't want to think about the implications of that.

'I assume you acquired his jacket for a reason,' said Nightingale.

'If we string police tape across our end of the platform people will come over to see if there's a body,' I said. 'If we string some yellow and black hazard tape instead, nobody will pay any attention except to grumble.' I held up the high visibility vest. 'This seals the deal and renders me invisible.'

'You've been taking lessons from Guleed again,' said Nightingale. 'Haven't you?'

'*Vestis virum reddit,*' I said – clothes make the man.

Nightingale looked blank.

'*Quintilianus,*' I said.

'Of course,' said Nightingale. 'Which reminds me, it's about time we started you on Greek.' My face must have betrayed my enthusiasm because he quickly added, 'I think you're going to find Marcus Aurelius particularly useful.'

'For what?' I asked.

Nightingale hesitated.

'Quoting, mainly,' he said. 'And thus maintaining an air of erudition and authority.'

'Given the fact that we're already working our arses off,' I said, 'do you really think that's an operational priority?'

'Undoubtedly,' said Nightingale. 'How else will we keep Abigail's respect?'

It was such a good plan, not exactly foolproof but you know, a solid, workmanlike, get-the-job-done sort of plan. It would have been nice if it hadn't started to go wrong in less than twenty minutes. The first southbound train was the very first train of the day and came in at about half five. By that time we were ready with our hazard tape and a stone that me and Nightingale had spent the previous evening imbuing with magic. We'd tried to keep the resultant *vestigia* as bland as possible but for some reason it smelt of coffee, stale beer and dusty curtains.

We'd dubbed it the *Hangover Stone*.

Nightingale said the freshness of the *vestigia* should be enough to attract any ghosts, but just to be on the safe side we planned to top it up with a low grade werelight as each southbound train approached.

At Jaget's suggestion we'd strung a second line of tape a couple of metres further up the platform so that people wouldn't be looking over our shoulders. Jaget, in his own BTP issue, high visibility vest loitered so we could concentrate on the task at hand. I handed him the anti-quated Leica camera and made him designated camera man in case we actually caught a ghost. The Leica was old enough to have a manual winding mechanism but Jaget assured me he could handle it.

'You should see some of the gear that's still in opera-tion on the Tube,' he said. 'This is practically high tech.'

The first southbound train was due in shortly and already the platform was about a third full of people drinking coffee out of cardboard cups and really wishing they weren't on their way to work. One or two close to us glared blearily in our direction, but it really was far too early in the morning for curiosity.

Jaget took a couple of pictures of the sleeping Toby to check the camera. Nightingale checked the destination board.

'Two minutes,' he said.

I blew on my fingers to warm them up and flexed them a bit before casting a werelight so low down the visible spectrum it was practically invisible and, more importantly, very localised. Then I turned to the Hangover Stone which was, in fact, a half brick nicked from some builder's rubble in the Folly's base-ment. When I touched it with the werelight it quickly glowed a cherry red. I motioned Jaget over to take some pictures.

'I want to know whether that's real or not,' I said.

I cautiously poked it with my finger and there was no heat. So probably not.

'Don't play with it, Peter,' said Nightingale. 'The train is almost here.'

I joined Nightingale to stand between the stone and the commuters further up the platform.

The train was moving slowly by the time it reached our little party and the driver had plenty of time to stare curiously at us before remembering to bring his vehicle to a smooth stop. The doors opened and the early morn-ing zombies shambled in.

I glanced at Toby, who yawned again and gave me a hopeful look.

The doors closed and the train whined off in the direc-tion of work and despair.

Toby, realising that nothing in the sausage department

was going to be forthcoming, curled up and went back to sleep.

'That was a bit of an anti-climax,' I said.

'I wouldn't worry,' said a voice behind me. 'There's plenty more trains where that came from.'

I looked around, expecting a member of the public. But instead a ghost stepped into existence like someone walking into the light of a campfire. He was a tall, thin white man in a navy pinstripe suit and a bowler hat. He carried a full length furled umbrella and a rolled up newspaper under his arm. He was faded and see-through in the daylight – an impression? An interpretation of the mind's eye? Or were real photons bouncing off something – however intangible? I heard a click and a whirr as Jaget took some shots with the antique Leica. He was using a very fast film so perhaps we'd settle that question.

Although, going by our past record, I wasn't going to hold my breath.

The ghost waved his umbrella at Nightingale.

'You, sir,' he said. 'Are you responsible for this delightful scene?'

'Can I help you?' said Nightingale.

'You could oblige me by continuing much as you are,' he said and stretched out his hands as if warming them against a fire. The palms and fingers, I saw, became increasingly solid as they approached the Hangover Stone. I made a mental note to check the photographs to see whether that was a true physical phenomenon or not. 'Things have been growing rather thin of late.'

'Glad to be of service,' said Nightingale and formally introduced the three of us to the ghost.

'Name of Mr Ponderstep,' said the ghost.

Because we were police we couldn't just leave it at a name – although no first name, I noticed – we always have to get an address, occupation, National Insurance number[3], previous convictions, inside leg measurement, favourite Pokémon . . . Mr Ponderstep didn't mind, he said, as long as we kept the magic flowing. He lived, or rather had lived, in West Drayton back when Harrow was hardly part of London at all. He'd caught the seven-fifteen into town each weekday morning, where he'd worked as a merchant banker.

When I tracked his records down much later, I discovered he'd fought at the Somme as an infantry lieutenant and had been awarded the Military Cross for conspicuous gallantry in the face of the enemy. He mentioned none of this during our conversation but Nightingale warned me against attributing this to ghostly incompleteness.

'People didn't talk about the Great War back then,' he said – not even when they were dead.

He did talk about his wife, his daughter and Splinter, his golden retriever. In fact it was quite hard to shut him up, even when the next southbound train pulled in – noticeably short on ghostly riders.

Not so the Hangover Stone, because we turned back from the departing train to find a transparent figure in riding boots, a rain cape and a tricorn hat had joined Mr Ponderstep.

'So, who are you?' I asked.

'I am but a humble road agent,' said the ghost. 'Cut unkindly short through the actions of jealous and unchristian men.' He slapped a hand theatrically to his

[3] Note for Reynolds: what you'd call a Social Security Number.

chest. 'Shot through the heart not more than half a mile from this very spot.'

'Do you have a name?'

'They call me Black Tom,' he said, and I made a note.

Black Tom held out his hands palm first towards the Hangover Stone.

'Splendid,' he said. 'The nights can be so chill. Strange to meet such a fine company out here amongst the clowns, but then the city has become very strange of late.'

'How so?' asked Nightingale.

'Why, the coaches run on iron tracks,' he said. 'And at such speeds a man might despair of making an interception.'

I looked over at Nightingale who shrugged.

'With hindsight,' he said, 'we really should have anticipated this problem.'

When a third ghost – a morose, thankfully silent, young man in frock coat and top hat – joined us it became clear that soon the entire ghost population of Harrow was likely to line up at our psychic soup kitchen.

'Psychic soup kitchen,' said Jaget who was still snapping away. 'Good one.'

'Go easy with the camera, Jaget,' I said. 'That film's hard to come by.'

Nightingale decided that he'd find a nice secluded spot away from the station and stage an all-you-can-eat magic buffet for the local ghosts. As they trailed hopefully after him, the three ghosts vanished into the morning sunlight. But I swear I could still hear Mr Ponderstep talking about his wife's Sunday brisket, heading up the stairs to the station concourse.

Toby didn't so much as look up to watch them go. He slept through the arrival and departure of the next two trains, but on the third he leapt to his feet and stared intently as it rolled into the station.

'Finally,' I said and Toby whined. I wasn't sure I liked his anxious tone, but if this was our train then at least we could slope off for refs afterwards.

The rush hour was in full flush and the platform was rammed. Travellers were pushing up against our first line of tape and glaring at Jaget because he was blocking their access to their habitual carriage door. We'd arranged the tape so that anyone getting off at our end, including actual alive people, could filter out.

We didn't see our girl at first, just heard a young voice cry, 'Doggie!'

Toby's head snapped around to look at the closest train door; I followed his gaze and saw her. She was young, white and dressed in late Victorian style – a white pinafore over a dark coloured dress and a wide brimmed straw hat. She was too transparent to be sure of any colours, but I thought her eyes were blue and her hair blonde.

She skipped off the train, ducked under our tape and, laughing, made a dash for Toby. He in turn pulled his head loose from his collar with suspicious ease and bolted up the platform. The ghost girl totally ignored our carefully crafted magical lure and chased after him. Exeunt dog pursued by ghost.

At the high point of rush hour in Harrow station there's no appreciable gap between a train leaving and a platform filling up, so that even as I started after them I saw Toby and the ghost girl vanish into a thicket of grumpy commuters. Fortunately, despite them all looking like a sack full of misery, the travellers knew which side the next train was due, so I cut across to the relatively-empty other platform and ran up that.

Harrow on the Hill has an elevated concourse built over the tracks through which the commuters trudged like extras from *Metropolis*. As I ran up the stairs I waved my warrant card and shouted 'Police! Police!'

The crowd parted in front of me in reluctant confusion with, I estimate, a third wondering who I was chasing, a third wondering why the police were chasing me and the last third thinking *Last thing I need first thing in the morning.*

At the top I saw Toby slip under the ticket barrier and got a barest flicker of a sense of movement that indicated the ghost girl was following. I didn't have time to alert the London Underground staff, so I vaulted the barrier and hoped they believed me when I shouted police again.

Someone yelled 'Oi' behind me, but I had Toby in my sights as he streaked between the legs of the commuters and down the stairs towards the street. Here the bland 1930s art deco stylings of the station gave way to the horror that was the 1980s where every public building was deliberately crafted to look as much like a urinal as possible. I've got longer legs than Toby, so I went down stairs faster than he did – still catching flickers of movement that I assumed was the ghost. A short barren indoor shopping precinct led to the main road which Toby crossed at full speed.

Presumably the ghost wasn't worried about the traffic, but I was. I had to slow down and watch in frustration as

Toby raced into the shapeless red brick pile that was the St Anne's shopping centre. I made up the lead coming down the stairs into the shopping centre's central atrium and was right behind them when Toby made the mistake of running into WHSmith's and got himself cornered in the Back to School section. There he made his stand before a wall of brightly coloured folders and discounted plastic Ziploc school stationery kits – now with safely blunted plastic compasses.

Toby bared his teeth as the ghost, much more visible in the store's strip lighting, advanced with her hand held out.

'Good doggie,' she said. 'Don't be afraid.'

I slipped around until I was facing her. She didn't notice me – her whole focus was on Toby.

'Good boy,' she said, her face bright with excitement.

Toby snarled and then snapped at her hand.

The ghost snatched it back, as if being bitten was a real possibility, a look of confusion on her face.

Toby looked at me and then managed an impressive jump right into my arms. Once safely there he wriggled around until he could face the ghost and bare his teeth at her.

She looked on the verge of tears.

I told Toby to behave and gave the ghost my best winning smile.

'My name is Peter,' I said. 'What's yours?'

She looked longingly at Toby and then at my face.

'You're awfully brown,' she said. 'Are you from the Empire?'

'I'll tell you if you tell me your name,' I said. 'It's only polite.'

The girl gave me a dainty little curtsy. 'Alice Bowman at your service,' she said.

'Pleased to meet you,' I said and told her that my mum was from Sierra Leone, which she actually knew was in West Africa, which put her ahead of the bulk of the modern population.

'Are you really a policeman?' she asked. 'The master said I was to find a policeman or a magistrate but not a priest. Definitely not a priest.'

'I am most certainly a police officer,' I said and showed her my warrant card. 'Who is your master?'

'Not *my* master, silly,' said Alice. '*The* Master, the master of the palace.'

'And he wanted you to find a policeman?' I remembered the postboy looking for someone to deliver a message to. 'Did he want you to deliver a message?'

'He wanted me to tell you a story,' she said. 'I wish I had a doggie.'

'If you tell me the story I'll let you pet him,' I said, and decided not to worry about how I'd persuade Toby to allow it until I had the bloody story.

'Promise?'

I opened my mouth to say that, absolutely, I promised, no problem, but I couldn't bring myself to lie – which is very unlike me. Words have power in the demi-monde and breaking a promise is supposed to have consequences. Not that I've seen any verifiable proof of this, you understand, but better safe than sorry.

'Once he gets to know you,' I said, 'I'm sure he'll let you.'

That seemed to satisfy Alice, who nodded.

'What was the story about?' I asked.

'About a princess, of course,' she said. 'All the good stories are about princesses.'

I asked her to tell me the story, and she flopped down to sit cross-legged and then made it clear she wasn't going to start until I did the same. So down I went and I couldn't help noticing that my knees started complaining almost immediately. Toby made himself comfortable in my lap, yawned and pretended to go to sleep.

'This princess,' I said. 'Does she have a name?'

Alice shook her head.

'Do you know where she lives?'

'In a castle.'

'Do you know the name of the castle?'

'Do you,' asked Alice, 'want to hear this story or not?'

'Pray continue,' I said. My knees were now really beginning to ache – I don't think I'd sat cross-legged for so long since I was in primary school.

'Once upon a time . . .' said Alice.

There was a Princess who lived in an unfortunately unidentified Kingdom who was beautiful and, well, basically beautiful, and there was this wicked man who didn't like her. Alice didn't know why he didn't like the Princess or even why he was wicked, although he undoubtedly was.

Now the Princess liked to visit the people of her kingdom, particularly the sick and unhappy, leaving early in the morning and returning to her castle in the evening very tired from all the help she had been giving. She did not know that the Wicked Man – again nothing in the way of useful identification – had been watching her.

'He watched her go out in the morning and come

home every evening,' said Alice. 'And each time he saw her, he hated her more.'

His hatred grew so fierce that he could no longer bear to see her walk free in the sunlight and so he laid his plans against her. One morning he put a magic potion in her tea and she fell into a swoon. While she slept he turned himself into dog and carried her away to his evil lair and threw her into his deepest darkest dungeon.

But the Wicked Man didn't know that right next to his dungeon lived the Master and all his friends in a splendid fairy palace made all of glass. The Master showed the Princess how to open the secret door to the palace and while the Wicked Man wasn't looking she slipped inside.

'Does the Master have a name?' I asked.

Alice shook her head emphatically and as she did I saw a crack appear in her neck and run down under her collar. It was a very fine break and Alice didn't seem to notice, but I remembered the postboy and figured I didn't have much time left. I asked whether the Princess was stuck in the fairy palace and Alice said she wasn't stuck exactly, but the only way out was through the dungeon and that was locked from the outside.

'The Master says that someone must be dispatched to save the Princess without delay,' said Alice. 'Sir William said he wasn't afraid to go but no help came so Tommy and Frenchie said they would, and then Clifford and Elizabeth, and then it was my turn. There was a spray of fine cracks at the corners of her eyes and mouth. 'There, that is my story and now I claim my reward.' She gave me a hopeful smile.

I was wondering how to persuade Toby to submit to

ghostly petting when a look of dismay passed across Alice's face.

'Oh,' she said and stood up. 'I think my time is over.'

'No,' I said and, standing, brandished a squirming Toby at her. 'Don't go.'

'Nanny says I should be brave and that Mummy and Daddy are waiting for me in heaven,' she said and then leant forward to confide a secret. 'But do you know what's curious? I think Nanny's talking rubbish. I don't think anybody knows what happens after you die. There, I said it. Die, die, die, death, death, death.' She giggled and hiccupped and looked serious again. 'Perhaps it's just another world, maybe, perhaps you go somewhere that's like this world only better. What do you think?'

I know what my mum believes and I know what I believe, but in a situation like this it isn't about your personal convictions. It's about what the person standing on the edge needs.

'My father believes that everything is music,' I said. 'And when you pass on you become part of the tune.' One improvisation amongst the millions and millions of melodies that create the symphony of everything. My dad basically believes that your life is your one chance at a solo – so it better be a good one. Mind you, he also thinks that Miles Davis was the Second Coming and most of the world's woes are due to humanity's failure to recognise him as such.

'I only know one song off by heart,' said Alice. 'Would you like to hear it?'

There were fine lines of darkness spreading across her face and across the crisp white front of her pinafore. It looked like the cracked pattern of parched mud.

I considered trying a werelight but I doubted that would help.

'Yes, please,' I said, and Alice began to sing.

A quarter tone flat as it happens, but beautiful all the same.

I didn't recognise the song at first. The tune and the structure of the couplets seemed familiar but it was only when she sang the fourth couplet –

Oranges and Lemons
Ring the bells at St Clement's

– that I recognised it as the nursery rhyme. An older version, I discovered later, after a bit of Googling.

As she sang her happy little song of legally enforced debt and credit avoidance she turned to dust, dissolving in front of me and drifting away on a non-existent breeze across the rows of Topsy and Tim books and the serried ranks of coloured pens.

I personally would have liked to believe that a friendly skeleton on a white horse was waiting to carry her off. Preferably to somewhere a good voice coach could teach her to sing on key. But I've always believed that my dad is right about one thing – your life is your solo and whatever song you choose to sing you only get to do it once.

Although if you're lucky you get to change the tune a couple of times.

Nightingale was waiting for me outside the shop. He frowned when he saw me.

'Is something wrong, Peter?'

'I think someone's been kidnapped,' I said.

5

The Water Baby

When in doubt, do police work. You start with the facts you've got and work your way methodically from there. Even if some of the facts come from an unorthodox source and your Day Book reads like an extract from a Bram Stoker novel.

There was a princess trapped in a dungeon . . .

'And you believe that represents a kidnapping?' said Nightingale.

Despite everything, we kept the Hangover Stone going until rush hour was well over because it's not good police work to assume there was only one ghost commuter per morning.

'There's a sentence you don't hear every day,' said Jaget.

'Speak for yourself,' I said.

After which we packed up and retired to a nearby pub for refs and regrouping.

'We can't be sure it's a kidnapping,' I said. 'But if it *is* a kidnapping we can't afford to delay for confirmation.'

Nightingale and Jaget nodded over their pints. Kidnappings were time sensitive, so you couldn't afford to mess about.

So, assuming it was one . . . we needed to know who

the victim was and where they were being kept.

'Alice Bowman said that the Master was sending her and her friends down the line, which I think means the "dungeon" has to be close to one of the stations further up.'

Jaget said in that case we could rule out Amersham because Alice had got off the direct Chesham train. 'Can we check Abigail's notes to see if all the sightings were on Chesham trains?' he asked.

'As soon as we get back to the Folly,' I said.

'Likewise we want to check with NCA's misper unit,' said Jaget. 'Start looking for missing women from further up the line.'

'What does a dungeon sound like to you?' I asked.

'A basement maybe?' said Jaget. 'And the description of our Princess's day sounds like someone commuting into work.'

'This could explain why the ghosts are so assiduously taking the morning train,' said Nightingale. 'They may be following a trail worn smooth by the victim.'

'Ghosts do that?' asked Jaget.

'I don't know,' he said. 'I'm going to have to check the literature. I'm also interested in this fairy castle that Alice spoke of. I believe a rummage in the magical library is called for.'

I pointed out that Abigail would be waiting for us when we got back to the Folly, was no doubt leading Molly astray even as we spoke.

'Abigail can join me in my search,' said Nightingale.

'Abigail?'

'Of course,' said Nightingale. 'Not only will it be good

practice for her Latin but it would be useful for her to gain some perspective on the craft.'

Nightingale has always been reluctant to let me loose on the library and I must have frowned or something because he went on, 'My worry with you, Peter, is not what you would learn but that, should you go into the library, you might never emerge again. Abigail can, at least, be lured back out with the promise of the pictures Jaget took.'

'She did describe it as a fairy palace,' I said. 'We might be looking at an incursion by the Fair Folk.' That being what the old literature called the type of *fae* that hung about looking cool and riding unicorns and, to my certain knowledge, stealing children. I explained a bit of this to Jaget who gave me the 'if you say so' look that had become very familiar to me since I joined the Folly.

'I can check the CP logbooks for the same geographical areas as we check for mispers,' I said. 'See if anything pops.'

'Leaving me to the mispers search,' said Jaget.

'Would you?' I said. 'That would be brilliant.'

So, our actions suitably assigned, we finished our drinks and got down to what passes for real policing at the Special Assessment Unit. We dropped Jaget off at BTP HQ so he could use his own secure terminal and, importantly, give the impression to his senior officers that he was hard at it. When we returned to the Folly we found Abigail in the kitchen teaching Molly how to take pictures of her food using an antiquated Samsung I suspected she'd liberated from my supply of expendable technology.

I suspected Molly wanted the pictures to send to her

friends on Twitter and Facebook, the ones that I was not supposed to know about. I didn't dare ask because we have an unspoken agreement – I don't question what she does on my computer when I'm out and, in return, she doesn't murder me in my sleep.

Back in the old days, before the Folly became a de facto branch of the Metropolitan Police – a time that the rest of the Met don't like to talk about – it was a much wider, grander organisation. A combination Gentlemen's Club, Royal Society and the unofficial magical arm of the British establishment. Back then, every county had an official County Practitioner who was there to keep the peace and deal with any problems that went beyond the purview of the local magistrates. The County Practitioners were utterly respectable and so integrated into the provincial gentry that I'm amazed that one never turned up in a Miss Marple mystery. Maybe some characters are too twisty – even for Agatha.

The CPs, as they were known, kept a working diary not unlike my own Day Book for keeping track of supernatural incidents. At the end of every calendar year they were supposed to be sent back to the Folly where, as far as I could tell, they were shelved at the back of the mundane library and never, ever, picked up again. Sometime after the First World War some bright spark decided that their contents should be neatly typed out, with carbon duplicates, categorised in various different ways and the results filed in a bank of green metal filing cabinets that lined an access corridor, also never to be picked up again. Nightingale said that at one time the Folly had had its own typing pool in the basement with the cooks and maids and Molly.

These are the only CP logs that are filed under subject as well as date, so I always start with them. Usefully, the area I was interested in had been part of Middlesex in those days, which narrowed it down further. The carbon copies are filed in cardboard folders tied up with ribbons and they felt dry and fragile under my fingertips. From 1921 the Middlesex County Practitioner had been one Wallace Blair Esq. from Arbroath of all places and who, by the standards of the Folly, had a nice succinct style. In the files marked 'F' for 'Fae' I found six promising reports of which one from May 1924 stood out.

```
Called out to Waterside, a village in the
parish of Chesham, today. The local rever-
end, who I know to be a sound man, said there
had been reports of figures dancing upon the
moor. Spoke to witnesses who claimed to
have seen six or so girls dancing in what
he described as 'nightwear and bloomers'.
This area has long been reputed to be the
abode of 'fairies'. Checked the logs of
my predecessors and found many references
including a verified abduction in 1852, in
this case foiled by Walter Buckland who is
rusticated at the old parsonage. Alas he
left no notes back at Russell Square.
```

And, also alas, Blair didn't say which previous CP's notes he'd consulted. So, short of ploughing through two hundred years of paperwork, I was stuffed. Blair found no direct sign of fairy involvement but did report *strong vestigia of the country type* which I took to mean possibly fairy. He also discovered bare footprints and some empty gin bottles – freshly emptied by the smell – and concluded that the dancers were probably women from the local mill out for a drunken lark. There followed a paragraph or three lamenting the decline of modern female morality which he blamed on allowing women to do factory work during the Great War. I bet that went down well with the typing pool.

It wasn't much, but then all I'd had in Herefordshire were imaginary friends and UFO sightings. So I did a quick Google and found the area around Waterside had had its share of sightings – lights in the sky in 2009 and a purported YouTube video of a spacecraft a couple of years later.

More importantly, Waterside was within a brisk cycle ride or short car journey from two stations on the Metropolitan Line – Chesham, and Chalfont & Latimer. So I hopped in the Blue Asbo and set forth to brave the wilds of Buckinghamshire.

Once you're past the M25 and driving up the Latimer Road there's no disguising that you're in a river valley and that Jaget's fabled good Tamil restaurants are a long way behind you. It didn't help that the woods and hedgerows were giving me flashbacks to Herefordshire, although thankfully it wasn't so hot and, hopefully, was lacking in psychopathic unicorns.

After a long stretch of mixed woods and farming, the valley narrows, you pass a sewage treatment plant, some heavy farming and some light engineering and you've arrived in Waterside. Beyond the recreation centre and swimming pool was the Moor – note capital letter.

Which, if you were looking for a wild and romantic place, was a bit of a disappointment in that it wasn't really a moor. It was in fact a marshy artificial island created in the tenth century by Lady Elgiva. Whoever she was, she presumably liked marshy islands for the waterfowl hunting and peasant drowning opportunities. It was used as a recreation area and had a car park, which was handy. So I parked up and had a sniff around. It was a triangular piece of land, hemmed in by the River Chess on one side and the Metropolitan Line on the other. The *high fae,* aka the *fair folk* aka *elves* or whatever you want to call them, do not live amongst us in the same way other *fae* do, but appear to exist parallel to our world. I'd use the phrase *other dimension* but I'm not ready to think about the implications of that just yet, thank you very much.

The *vestigia* they leave behind during an incursion are subtle but powerful, and if they'd been abducting princesses in the vicinity I was pretty certain I'd spot it. I checked around to make sure nobody was watching me then lay down in the long grass and pressed my ear to the ground.

For a long time there was nothing but the sweetish smell of grass, the swish of passing cars and the vague worry that I hadn't remembered to back-up my current set of case notes. I've learnt to allow myself to let go of these things and exist in the now – which is exactly as easy as it sounds.

Very faintly I caught the distant regular thumping of old machinery, the crackle of paper and an acrid, caustic stink. There'd been mills all along this stretch of the river. The girls the prim and proper Wallace Blair had suspected of drunkenly dancing through the night had worked in those mills and lived in the mean terraces on the opposite bank.

But there was none of the deep vibrato sense of change that you got from an incursion. I suspected it *had* been gin-drinking working girls back in 1924 and nothing magical before or after. I raised my head to look over at the river.

At least nothing fae.

There was a well maintained and tree-shaded path running alongside the water. I cast an experienced eye over the suspiciously new looking reed beds and anti-erosion fixtures. They call this sort of scheme 'rewilding'. I can't prove that a sudden rush to improve your local river indicates the emergence of young and active genius loci. But when Mama Thames went into the river at London Bridge it was so toxic that drowning was the least of your worries. And now it's cleanest industrial river in Europe. Just saying.

Right on cue a sturdy little white boy came running down the path towards me waving his arms and yelling. He didn't look more than four or five, with amazingly pink cheeks, fair hair and blue eyes. He was dressed in red shorts, a stripy blue and green T-shirt and blue trainers. As soon as I saw him I automatically started scanning for nearby traffic in case he ran into the road, potential child abductors and/or responsible adults.

I soon spotted an elderly white couple, a man and a woman, twenty metres behind him and trying to muster the speed to catch up. The man, grey haired, tweed jacketed and carrying a walking stick, looked dangerously out of breath and I resolved to gently corral the boy to a stop and return him to – what? Grandparents, at a guess.

I bent down and opened my arms to block the pavement, which the boy took as a cue to throw himself at me and wrap his arms around my neck. It was like plunging my face into an icy stream, shocking and exciting and with that the grinding of metal teeth and the fluttering sound of paper wings. I stood up and hoisted him onto my hip.

'What's your name?' he cried.

'Peter,' I said. 'What's yours?'

'I'm Chess,' he said. 'Which is supposed to be short for Chester.'

The grandfather had been forced to stop for a bit of a breather, but the gran was made of sterner stuff.

'Chester,' she said as she approached. 'Put that poor man down.' And then to me, 'I'm so sorry. He seems to have got away from us.' She glanced back at the man who stopped coughing long enough to raise a reassuring hand.

I assured her that it was fine and that I was skilled in the ways of wrangling children, having a ton of nieces, nephews and assorted cousins.

'You smell funny,' said Chester.

A look of total mortification crossed the woman's face.

'Chester!' she said, and looked at me with a pleading expression. 'I'm so very very sorry.'

I told her not to worry, even as Chester asked me if I ate funny food.

'Here, let me take him,' said the woman. She sagged as I handed him back. He was a heavy little boy and slid down her front until he was standing on the pavement holding her hand.

'I'm so very sorry,' said the woman.

The old man arrived in time to catch the fag end of the conversation. He eyed me belligerently and said, 'He's just a boy.'

'And a handsome one too,' I said, because no parent or grandparent, however loco, can resist flattery aimed at their offspring. I asked how old he was and the old man and woman exchanged strangely nervous looks before saying that he was four.

I said that he was a big lad for four, but again the couple's reaction was all wrong. Alluding to a big healthy child is normally taken as a compliment, but they started to back off in a defensive fashion that is totally familiar to anyone who's spent five minutes in law enforcement. I couldn't let them walk away, given who or what I thought the child might be, so I adopted my most positive customer-facing voice.

'Hi,' I said, 'I'm with the Metropolitan Police. I wonder—' But I never got to finish, because the woman's hands flew to her face and the man started shouting, 'No, no, no! You can't have him.'

'Why would I want him?' I asked.

The man and woman stared at each other and I had the awful realisation that if I hadn't been suspicious enough to intervene before, I was well and truly over that line now.

The old man seized the boy's hand and started dragging him back up the path.

'Come on, Chester,' he said. 'It's time for us to go home.'

'But I want to stay with the police man,' said Chester, showing his age.

'No, no, no,' said the old man. 'It's time for tea.'

The boy was resisting, not yanking his arm back or digging his heels in, but definitely resisting the old man's pull.

'Allen,' called the old woman. 'What are you doing? It's too late. Allen!' She turned to me and I saw that she was crying, proper old-fashioned stiff upper lip tears. 'I suppose we knew this day would happen. I just hoped we would have more time.'

When faced with complex and inexplicable circumstances, a modern police officer will fall back onto one of two basic policing approaches. Option one; call for backup, arrest everyone in the vicinity and sort it out down the nick. Or option two; locate the nearest source of tea, sit everyone down and hope nobody's carrying a concealed weapon.

I went for option two, although I did keep an eye on the old man's walking stick all the way back to their house – just in case. Their names were Allen and Lillian Heywood and they lived in a two bedroom Edwardian terrace further down the street opposite the community swimming pool and recreation centre. The house was neat and well cared for, but to my eye the Heywoods were losing the battle against the four-year-old agent of entropy who was living with them. There was grime building up in the seams and corners of the hallway and the walls bore a line of gunge at hip level.

The Heywoods might have been aware of this, because they quickly led me through the kitchen, worn but clean, and out into the modest garden at the back. This was well maintained but strewn with the array of discarded action figures, deflated balls and other forsaken toys that I expected. At the far end was a low fence and, also as I expected, beyond that a metre and a half of grass bank before the course of the River Chess.

Chess insisted on taking my hand and dragging me out to see his river. What had once been a culverted course had been smothered by more of the cultivated reed banks. No doubt all the microorganisms and miniature water life that Bev says are so vital for a healthy river were sucking up nutrients to their hearts' content before becoming snacks for the next organism in the great chain of life. Although Bev says it's more of a web, shunting various forms of energy around the ecosystem. Waving the gauntlet of self-organising complexity in the face of entropy itself.

I told Chess that his was a lovely river and in fact quite the nicest river I'd ever seen and, content, he led me back to the white plastic garden table and chairs for tea and explanations.

'We found him two years ago,' said Mrs Heywood. 'There was a terrible rainstorm one night and Allen was worried that the river would flood, so he kept going outside with a torch to check. And then, just after midnight, he comes back into the kitchen with this poor mite.'

'I found him standing at the end of the garden,' said Mr Heywood. 'Totally starkers.'

This had led to rushing him into the house, wrapping him in a blanket and plying him with hot chocolate made with full milk, naturally.

'Naturally,' I said.

Obviously after that they had planned to call the police, honest, only it was such a dreadful night and what with the flooding and the chaos they thought the police might be busy.

'Plenty of time to call them in the morning,' said Allen.

But in the morning there was breakfast to make and clearing the muck off the flooded bit of the garden, which Chess helped with, and the next thing they knew it was evening and the poor little mite had curled up and gone to sleep on the sofa.

'When did you decide to keep him?' I asked.

Lillian paused in the act of offering me a teacake we were on to tea and cakes by then.

'We didn't decide,' she said. 'Not as such.'

'We more sort of didn't try to get rid of him,' said Allen.

I took a teacake, as did Chess, who proceeded to try to stuff as much of it into his mouth in one go as he could. The logistics of keeping him were surprisingly easy; they merely told everyone that Chess was a great nephew of theirs and they were looking after him. They let their neighbours assume that something vaguely *Daily Mail*-ish had happened to the parents – drug addiction, mental breakdown, something like that, and got on with the practical side of raising a lively young boy.

'You couldn't have got away with something like that in the old days,' said Lillian. 'Could you, Allen?'

'No,' said Allen.

In the old days everybody in a village like Chesham knew everybody else and everybody knew everybody's business. Somebody would have asked questions and sooner or later the vicar would have popped around for a 'little chat'.

'Likely it would have been that young feller,' said Allen. 'The one that went on to be bishop.' This being the 1950s when there were three separate parishes covering Chesham proper – Waterside where Allen and Lillian lived, Latimer and Ashley Green.

'The funny thing is,' said Allen, 'that the more people who live here, the less religion there seems to be.'

A certain river goddess of my acquaintance says that the late Victorian church was less than happy to share turf with 'pagan' spirits, particularly in urban areas. I looked over at Chess who took that as a cue to show me how wide he could open his mouth to display masticated teacake.

I could understand their point of view.

Lillian and Allen were old Waterside – their families had been living in the area since before the Mills were built. I wondered if there was a connection and I wondered how old Chess was going to have to get before I could ask him.

'We fell into a routine,' said Lillian, although they had wondered how they were going to register Chess for school when the time came. There being a serious absence of birth certificates and other official whatnots.

'We would have loved some help,' said Lillian. 'But we didn't know where to turn.'

'Everybody else seems to have a line to call,' said Allen. 'Or a something-or-other on the internet.'

They paused and looked at me.

To avoid their gaze, I looked around the garden which, unlike the house, was lush and blooming. What I thought were probably roses climbed up and around the kitchen door. A fat bumble bee nosed around the cab of a red and yellow Tonka truck before zigzagging lazily off amongst nodding ranks of orange, yellow and blue flowers. There was a drowsy quiet about the garden. I couldn't hear the cars going past at the front, or the neighbour's radio. We could have been in the middle of an ancient forest with the oak and ash and willow tree.

I looked sharply at Chess, who gave me a wide smile with just a hint of sly about the corners.

I mentally sang the sad lament of the hard pressed copper.

Oh for I am not a social worker that these woes are placed upon my care.

'Stop that,' I told Chess, who giggled.

This would have to be sorted out, but not this afternoon.

'I'm not promising anything,' I said. 'But I'll see if I can arrange some assistance.'

They both looked stricken. Not social services, they said.

I had considered them, but what had Buckingham Social Services ever done to me that I was going to inflict a cheeky little godlet on them? I told Lillian and Allen I'd be in contact within a week and they were not to worry. At the very least, I thought, I can arrange a competent cleaner to come in and scrub out some of those corners.

Before I left I asked Chess whether he'd noticed anything strange recently. Given his age I thought it was unlikely. He looked up at me with his big pink face and casually pointed upstream.

'There,' he said. 'Spooky stuff.'

'Really,' I said. 'What kind of spooky stuff?'

His face screwed up in concentration,

'Don't know,' he said. 'It's loud. Lots of shouting.'

'Can you hear what they're shouting about?'

He shook his head.

'How long have they been shouting for?'

'Forever and ever,' said Chess, and went back to his game.

When you're four, forever and ever can mean yesterday. But amongst my other policing skills I've acquired a proficiency in straw-clutching that verges on the savant. So I checked Google Maps on my phone and found that Chesham was upstream, the last stop on that branch of the Metropolitan Line and the furthest station out from London.

Jaget called me as I headed back for the Asbo and said he'd found a couple of likely candidates amongst the misper files.

'Did one of them live in Chesham?' I asked.

'As it happens,' he said, 'yeah. Name of Brené Mc-Claren. Lives in Chesham, commutes into London where she works for Islington Council as a social worker.'

And the princess liked to visit the people of the kingdom, I thought, *especially the sick and unhappy.*

'I think we've found our primary focus,' I said.

6

The Ghost Wrangler

B ut not our only one, because the first rule of good policing means not haring down the first lead you get, however promising, until you've at least made a stab at eliminating the alternatives. Since, like our Brené McClaren, the alternatives – one from Amersham and the other from Rickmansworth – both fell into the jurisdiction of the Thames Valley Police, we would achieve this through the application of the second rule of good policing which is: always try to get someone else to do the grunt work.

In this instance this was the aforementioned Thames Valley Police, who have about the same relationship with the Met as Everton FC has with Liverpool[4]. Although these days both sides try to keep it professional when cooperating on a case. Jaget set up a meeting with the local plod in charge and hopped on the next train up – I agreed to meet him at Chesham station.

Chesham is where the Metropolitan Line flounders to a stop and you could feel the town vacillating between being nothing more than a dormitory for

---

[4] Note for Reynolds: Like the Yankees and the Red Sox only with added sectarianism.

London commuters and a county market town with a cookie cutter pedestrianised high street. It's the sort of white-bread rural ideal with good communication links favoured by media types who feel that they've done their bit for urban multiculturalism and are looking for somewhere comfortably vanilla to raise their kids.

The valley of the Chess narrows as it reaches the town and the station is one of those that ends up halfway up the side of the hill with a couple of steep roads down into the town centre. The station has the big car park and stuffed bicycle rack that is the proud mark of a commuter town but, alas, not the coffee shop that is the true sign of civilisation. Not even one of those kiosk things which, I know from bitter experience, are a bastard to work in. I asked around and was told that all the cafés were on the High Street at the bottom of a steep hill. So I called Bev instead and chatted to her while I waited for Jaget.

'And he was, what, about four?' she said.

'The paediatrician they went to thought he was about two when they first had him checked out,' I said.

Beverley was amazed the doctor hadn't reported them.

'They went private,' I said. 'Hinted that he was Romanian.'

'Clever,' said Beverley. 'I like them already.'

'Yeah,' I said. 'But they're in over their heads and I'm not even sure our little water baby isn't using the influence on them. Which is, one might consider, a bit of an ethical dilemma.'

'Sounds a bit mythic to me,' she said. 'Childless couple, foundling baby.' There was a pause and I heard a young woman's voice asking a question. Then Bev came back on. 'Chelsea wants to know if he strangled any snakes.'

I said that I'd be sure to ask at the next interview.

'The Chess isn't my watershed, it's not even my Mum's watershed,' said Beverley. 'Or the Old Man's for that matter. It's probably not a good idea for me to get involved.'

I said that she'd been fast enough to get involved in Herefordshire, but she said that was different.

'That was a favour. I had permission. There was mutual subsidiarity and all that style of thing.'

'I don't think that word means what you think it means,' I said.

'It's the principle that central authority only acts when a problem can't be solved at a local level,' said Bev, which shut me up – even though I still don't think she was using the word right. Fortunately just then I saw Jaget coming out of the station and had an excuse to ring off.

Our TVP liaison was one DS Malcom Transcombe out of Amersham nick. He was a short, stout, white man with thinning red hair in his late forties who looked upon us with the delighted eye of a man who's just had his workload doubled by a couple of likely lads from the big city.

He'd arranged to meet us in the car park to prove that he was a bit busy and could we get this out of the way quickly, and had arrived in a well-kept ten year old Rover 75 with a hideous purple custom spray job.

DS Transcombe leant back against the bonnet, crossed his arms and gave me and Jaget the eye.

'Where did you say your information came from?' he asked.

'Sources,' I said. 'We wouldn't have bothered you at this stage of the investigation, except it's a possible kidnapping . . .' I let that trail off.

'Sources?' said DS Transcombe, who was no doubt thinking of all the unpaid overtime this was going to cost him.

'Confidential sources.'

DS Transcombe narrowed his eyes. You see, the trouble with detectives is that they're detectives and are literally trained not to believe anything they haven't verified themselves. Plus about two seconds after Jaget contacted him he would have been on the phone to an 'old mate' in the Met. Every good police officer who wants to survive on the job for more than five minutes has a network of 'old mates'. Jaget is mine at the BTP. DS Transcombe would have phoned his, let's call him Bill, and asked just what the Special Assessment Unit is when it's at home and what should he do about them?

Bill, if he was any kind of an insider, would probably tell Transcombe the SAU was the latest name for the Folly, you know the guys that deal with the 'special cases'. You mean like . . . ? Yeah, those ones. So what am I supposed to do with them? Handle the case, keep your distance and kiss your clear-up rate goodbye. Oh well, thanks Bill, that was helpful. Anything for an old mate – you know that.

'Right,' said DS Transcombe, dragging out the word. 'Sources.'

See, a reputation, even a dubious one, can be a useful thing.

He asked what we wanted to do next and I asked what actions had been scheduled with regards to Brené

McClaren's disappearance and he said bugger all so far. He'd actioned a statement from the workmate who'd reported her missing and had been planning a visit to her house this very afternoon, as it happened.

'Good,' I said. 'Because I figured that would be a good start.' And anyway you don't go kicking down doors in someone else's manor without permission. 'Where is it?'

'Just down there,' said DS Transcombe, pointing back the way I'd come. 'Waterside.'

So we climbed back into our respective motors and drove down to what looked to me a particularly uninspired bit of late twentieth century social housing dropped into what had probably been a bit of brown field behind an original row of Victorian terraces. At least parking was convenient, with spaces along the frontage and then steps up to the balcony stroke walkway that is the defining feature of modern urbanism. Brené's house was the first in the row. We checked the front windows, but the net curtains were drawn and the inside was too dark to see. As a matter of course we rang the bell, banged on the door, yelled 'police' and, as a last resort, because we like our dignity, bent over to yell through the letter box.

DS Transcombe sighed and looked sourly at me.

'Bugger,' he said.

Forcing an entry is always a pain because, apart from anything else, modern doors are bloody hard to kick in and don't have the convenient small glass panels you can smash and reach in to lift the latch. Round the back is even worse because modern French windows are usually single sheets of plate glass and breaking one of those is hard to do safely. Now, Nightingale had been teaching me his useful little spell for popping a lock, but I'm not that proficient at it yet, and in any case if we were dealing with a magical abduction then I didn't want to contaminate the scene by laying down a new layer of *vestigia*.

Plus I wasn't so certain of DS Transcombe that I wanted to freak him out.

In the end Jaget visited the neighbours in turn until he found one that was keeping an emergency spare key for Brené. DS Transcombe took their name and details and told them we might be back to interview them later. Then we let ourselves in.

Nobody had been in the house for at least a couple of weeks. We all knew that from the moment we stepped over the pile of junk mail in the hallway. The mouldy breakfast washing up, the off milk in the fridge, the unmade bed with a thin layer of dust were all just confirmation. There's always a tension between the need to preserve a scene for modern forensics and the pressure to get a move on in a time-sensitive investigation. We figured we had to do an initial search, but we all put on our gloves and touched things as little as possible.

We discovered that Brené McClaren's passport was in a shoebox on the top shoe shelf in her wardrobe, there hadn't been a violent struggle, and she had terrible taste in music.

'What's wrong with Arcade Fire?' asked Jaget.

I did not dignify that with an answer.

We split up and did a quick canvass of the neighbours. It was late enough for everyone to be home from work, but nobody on her terrace had seen her for days, possibly weeks. I noticed DS Transcombe making a note – someone, several someones probably – was going to be doing a proper house-to-house just as soon as the overtime was sorted out.

'You think she was abducted on the way to work?' said DS Transcombe.

I pointed out the breakfast things, the unmade bed and the fact that it was a work colleague who had reported her missing. It was thin but it was a place to start – you can't wait for more data forever.

Despite having a driving licence, the DVLA showed no car registered in Brené's name. With that in mind, the three of us walked back towards the station to see what the fastest route was likely to be. It was Jaget, with his extensive knowledge of problem spots on the Underground, who knew about the public footpath.

'There's a couple of good points where people try and access the tracks,' he said.

I didn't ask why anybody would want to risk the electric two-step on the tracks because, as police, all three of us knew that there wasn't anything so stupid that somebody wouldn't try it sooner or later. Although these days there was likely to be some YouTube of them doing it, which at least helped with the post-mortem investigation.

As we traced the route, DS Transcombe made a note of where all the CCTV cameras were and which shops and houses should be in the first wave of door to door.

The actual footpath was practically dead straight and overshadowed by house backs on one side and trees on the other. By this time the sun was low enough for the path to be gloomy with occasional patches of evening sun.

'It's a good place to ambush someone,' I said as we walked its length.

'Nah,' said Jaget. 'First thing in the morning this path is going to be heaving.'

'Doesn't mean she wasn't snatched,' said DS Transcombe. 'People have been grabbed from crowds before.'

I was thinking of Alice's tale of how the Princess's tea had been drugged.

'Perhaps her attacker took her from her house before she could leave,' I said.

'One theory at a time,' said DS Transcombe, but we found no convenient holes in the chain-link fence that lined the side with the tracks, no abandoned bags or other signs of a struggle. Not even a dropped brooch or packet of lembas.

We stopped when we reached the station and then walked back a different route – just to be on the safe side. DS Transcombe had called his Inspector as soon as we'd left Brené McClaren's house and he called back just as we reached where our cars were parked.

'My governor says we're going to go all in,' said DS Transcombe. 'We want to see if we can catch the late news, put it out as an alert on social media.'

They were going to start house-to-house first thing, canvass commuters on the footpath and at the station. Then interview the work mates and check on ex-boyfriends, male relatives and all the usual suspects that the police look for when a woman goes missing. The media strategy was going to be helped by the fact that Brené was a good looking white woman in her late twenties, so coverage should be good and sightings numerous. Luckily it wasn't going to be my job to process them.

I told DS Transcombe that we'd let them know if we dug up anything at our end.

'Not so fast,' he said with a grin. 'My governor wants to see you first.'

*

I woke up to the smell of coffee and Abigail sitting on the end of my bed practically bouncing up and down with excitement.

'Guess what we found?' she said.

I blinked at Abigail and wondered where the coffee smell was coming from until I realised that Molly was standing right next to the bed and holding a breakfast tray. Only Molly can make breakfast in bed a sinister experience, but over the years I've managed to suppress my instinct to leap up screaming. It's not getting any easier though.

At least it was scrambled eggs on toast this time and not kippers.

I sat up, took the tray off her and watched her glide back out the door.

Abigail was smart enough to wait for me to drink some of the coffee, although she did nick a bit of my toast.

'Oi,' I said.

'Don't you want to know what it is?' she asked.

'What's the time?' I asked.

'Eight . . . ish,' she said.

Operation Polygon would be well up and running by now. The TVP would be questioning commuters as they arrived at Chesham Station with additional coverage at Chalfont & Latimer, and Amersham just to be on the safe side. Serious house-to-house would start after nine and cadaver dogs would be sniffing around likely dumping sights. TVP had made it clear that they would value my input from within the sphere of my core competences.

Which meant I really hoped Abigail had discovered something useful.

'We found a ghost wrangler,' said Abigail. 'Guess where?'

'Chesham,' I said.

'Points,' said Abigail, meaning yes. And also meaning she was going to draw this out as much as possible.

'Now or historical?' I asked.

'Oh, definitely historical,' said Abigail. 'George Buckland, born 1742 died 1815.'

'Don't tell me,' I said. 'At the Battle of Waterloo.'

'Nah – in bed.'

'And his relevance to this case is?'

'First,' said Abigail, 'there's got to be context – right?'

Because the parish of Chesham was unusual in that, at the time of King Harold, the church used to have three vicars, or rather the *advowson* for the parish was split equally between the three adjacent manors. Advowson is the right to appoint the incumbent clergy of a parish, so three advowsons meant three incumbents.

'Which was all right in those days,' said Abigail. 'Because they were mostly in it for the tithes.'

The three 'mates of Harold' passed the rights down to their descendants who all, at one time or another, and in a spirited attempt to avoid eternal damnation, passed them on to local monasteries who farmed them out to their favourites, political allies and/or misshapen sons of the abbot. Because while the monasteries often disagreed with the state about the authority of the king, they were bang on side for feudalism when it worked for them. However, three hundred years later the monasteries were done in by the Renaissance, the chill theological winds blowing in from Germany, and Henry VIII's need to get his leg over on a regular basis.

'Is this going to become relevant at any point?' I asked.

'Well, the advowsons bounced about between various posh families until one of them was picked up by a geezer called George Buckland,' said Abigail. 'And guess what he did for a living?'

'He was a vicar?'

'Wrong!' said Abigail, which apparently wasn't that unusual because being a country parson didn't actually involve much in the way of theology. 'He was a practitioner, wasn't he?'

George Buckland Esquire was not exactly a founder of the modern Folly, but was definitely around when it relocated to the nice Georgian pile I was currently eating my scrambled eggs in. He even belonged to the wild and woolly, and earlier, times when the practitioners of London met on a disreputable floating coffee house on the Thames. Back then a practitioner could consort with conmen, mountebanks and even, shockingly, women – and it was reputedly from a woman that he learnt how to capture ghosts.

'Ghosts?' I asked. 'How?'

'A lot of this is gossip, right?' said Abigail. 'But he was said to have married a creole lady from New Orleans and she knew how to make this thing called a rose jar. Which you're supposed to be able to catch a ghost in. But once you put the ghost in, you couldn't let it out because it would fall apart. The ghost, that is. Any of this ringing a bell?'

It was. And it might explain our disintegrating ghosts.

'Are you saying Brené McClaren is a practitioner?'

'Not really,' said Abigail, eyeing my last piece of toast. 'We ain't finished yet.'

Because George Buckland's membership of the all new officially sanctioned and respectable Society of the Wise, which was what the Folly was calling itself in those days, was not smooth.

'He's famously the first person to face a disciplinary tribunal,' said Abigail. 'Ever.'

'What for?'

Abigail grinned.

'Nobody knows,' she said. 'The records were sealed and Mr Nightingale says he can't find them.'

'Helpful,' I said.

'But not important right now,' said Abigail. 'What is important is that the parsonage stayed in the family until 1914 when his great grandson died without any kids.'

I thought I knew where we were going, but I kept my face suitably gormless so as not to harsh Abigail's squee. At least that's the story I'm going with.

'They never found the rose jars,' said Abigail.

And there are records of Walter Buckland, who was the last of the family to join the Folly, mentioning them in conversation as late as 1860.

Ah, I thought, Walter Buckland of the abducting Fairies fame.

'So what if they're still in the parsonage,' said Abigail. 'In the *basement*?'

I finished my coffee.

'Let's go and have a look,' I said.

'Yes, let's,' said Abigail.

7

The Polish Barista

We did pause to check whether we could find Walter Buckland's CP ledger first. Or rather I sent Abigail to do that, with the rare delight of a minion who has at last discovered that he has a littler minion to put upon. While she was doing that I called DS Transcombe and told him what we were planning, although strangely I didn't tell him it was bring-a-nosy-cousin-to-work day. He said he'd generate an action at his end and I made a note of the conversation in my day book just in case something went horribly wrong. Then, with everybody's arse suitably covered I picked Abigail up from the library and we piled into the Orange Asbo, which had the better engine, and headed off with a song in our hearts and an argument about music selection on our lips.

We finally compromised on Janelle Monáe and sang along to 'Many Moons' as we left the comforting boundary of the M25 behind.

The third parsonage, former home of George Buckland and his descendants, was built down the hill from the St Mary's Church on the wrong side of the busy A416. Convenient for the shops, though, I noticed.

'This is a mess,' I said when I saw it.

'I thought you liked old buildings,' said Abigail.

'Old doesn't always mean good,' I said. 'Case in point.'

I'm no expert, but I'd say the original was seventeenth century, erected during the period known as the great rebuilding when the gentry kicked their servants out of the hall and the simple folk finally turfed the livestock out of their living rooms. It was well built, I'll give it that. A lot of the original narrow red brickwork and a particularly fine Tudor chimney had survived, but its dimensions were as squat and as lumpen as Le Corbusier's imagination. Somebody had added a wing and additional chimneys in the neo-classical style, and a ground floor coated with ill thought out regency rustication was just the icing on the cake. At least the sash windows hadn't been replaced with PVC frames, although from the residents' point of view that probably just meant the house was both ugly and difficult to keep warm.

There was a grey intercom bolted onto the wall beside the front door with three slots for name tags, all with the factory default placeholder still in them.

While we didn't have a full Integrated Intelligence Platform report, we did have a list of the residents from the electoral register. I started with the top button and worked my way down. Only Geoffrey Toobin, in the ground floor flat, was at home. He was a pleasantly wide-faced white guy with a mop of brown hair and an unfortunate predilection for plaid shirts and skinny jeans.

He glanced at my warrant card and then gave Abigail a puzzled look.

'Aren't you a bit young to be a police woman?' he said.

'Yes,' she said. 'Yes, I am.'

I explained that she was a volunteer helping canvass the neighbourhood in the search for Brené McClaren, which was a good segue into whipping out my tablet and showing him her photograph.

'And she's missing?'

I explained that, indeed, she was missing and asked whether he recognised her, perhaps from his morning commute. He said he'd love to help but he was one of the residents of Chesham who didn't slog into the city each day. He was, in point of fact, a solicitor who worked out of an office in the town centre.

I asked whether he knew his neighbours in the other two flats and he said only to nod to and confirmed their names, or at least their first names. This was all a warm-up to me asking to have a look round his flat.

Given that he was a solicitor, I wasn't surprised that he gave it some thought before agreeing.

'It means we can tick you off the list,' I said.

'What list is that?' he asked.

'It consists of just about everybody who lives in the area,' I said.

'That's a lot of people,' he said, and I knew right then that he was our man.

I've never put much store in hunches and the detective's gut – even when it's mine – but if this had been a film there would have been a sinister string section playing away in the background.

Unfortunately the interior of Geoffrey Toobin's flat wasn't exactly awash with sinister objects, except maybe the hammered aluminium coffee table that was a serious breach of the peace in itself. It was a standard late-twenties single man's collection of mid-range flat pack, cheap stuff left over from uni[5] and the occasional antique that I suspected he'd inherited from his family.

The flat itself occupied all the ground floor that hadn't been retrofitted into an awkwardly shaped and dimly lit communal lobby. I'm probably not up to POLSA standards but I was pretty certain that there were no voids or hidden rooms on the ground floor. Geoffrey Toobin followed us from room to room with a quizzical expression carefully glued to his face. I made a point of making sure I was between him and Abigail at all times, which is exactly why you don't take teenaged relatives with you on a house-to-house.

We finished our tour in the communal lobby where I whispered to Abigail that she needed to go sit in the car. She trotted off with a docility that would have amazed every adult that had ever crossed her path. I asked Geoffrey Toobin some routine questions about his neighbours and when I judged that he had relaxed a bit I asked him about the basement.

'The basement?' he said.

'Yes, sir,' I said. 'A house of this type should have a basement or a cellar. Do you know where the stairs are?'

He hesitated – the bland look stayed, but if I'd needed any confirmation that was it.

Still, my personal confidence was not the same as your actual evidence and these days we're expected to provide the good stuff before we charge people. It's political correctness gone mad I tell you.

'There's nothing down there,' he said. 'But you can have a look if you want.'

---

5 Note for Reynolds: Uni is short for University.

'Thanks,' I said, and then stopped as if suddenly remembering something. 'Got to make a quick call.'

I called Nightingale and told him where I was.

'I've just got a basement to check,' I said. 'Then I can move on.'

Nightingale, who knew exactly what had led me to the parsonage, asked me whether there was a problem.

'Nah,' I said. 'I'll give you a call in five minutes when I've finished.'

'Understood,' said Nightingale, 'I'll let Jaget know. Would you like me to apprise Thames Valley Police?'

I said that wouldn't be a bad idea, and we hung up.

Satisfied that not only was backup on its way but that Geoffrey Toobin knew that too, I let him lead me to a white wooden door, tucked out of sight down a short side corridor, which gave us access to the basement.

I still made him go down the steps ahead of me.

The stairs were unusual – instead of your standard creaky wooden affair they were solid, built against the wall of the basement with stone risers and no handrail. It was also missing the traditional creepy 40 watt bulb. Instead there was modern LED strip lighting and whitewashed walls.

And nothing else.

No junk, old bicycles, partially disassembled motorbikes, manacles, Perspex cells or clever rope rigs for strangling Daniel Craig.

'This is a bit bare,' I said.

Geoffrey Toobin shrugged.

'It was like this when I bought it,' he said.

'When was that?'

'Two years ago,' he said. 'I didn't want to fill it up with

junk because it's a useful space, but even so it's not exactly somewhere you want to spend a lot of time.'

'You don't have any hobbies?' I asked. There was a faint whiff of bleach. Now, my mum's attitude to bleach is that if you haven't used up the entire bottle of Domestos equivalent, then you probably haven't cleaned the surfaces properly. So I've had a lot of experience with this smell, and someone had used a lot of bleach in the basement, but a while back. A week ago, maybe more – it was hard to tell in such an enclosed space.

'Tennis,' said Geoffrey Toobin. 'Not really a basement sport.'

There was a restless ringing sound like glass wind chimes and the smell of salt sea and rum and molasses – that was *vestigiu*.

'Have you finished? Because I really have some work that needs finishing up.'

'You're working from home today?'

'I . . .' he said and hesitated. 'I often work from home. My job's nearly all paperwork.'

It had been hard to tell through a thick layer of white paint, but the bricks in the far wall were laid in a different bond from the rest of basement. All of them were of a non-standard size, flatter and smaller than modern bricks – probably seventeenth or eighteenth century – but they'd definitely been re-laid and definitely no earlier than the mid-nineteenth.

'Given the size of the house, this basement seems a bit small,' I said. 'There isn't another area? Maybe accessed from outside or through a trap door?'

'I wouldn't know,' he said. 'Sorry.'

Again he was giving me fuck-all in the way of a response – either he was unnaturally calm or my gut was wrong.

Or, rare but horrible, some other entity had sequestrated him and was either puppeting him right now or had left him with no memories of his actions.

Or my gut was wrong.

Confirmation bias has put more innocent people in prison than malice.

'Well, thank you for your time,' I said and made sure I went up the stairs ahead of him.

Inconveniently, the stretch of the A416 outside the parsonage was a dual carriageway with no parking. I'd left the Asbo outside the Chesham Cottage Chinese restaurant across the way – it was the one place I could park and maintain a good view of the front door. If anything kicked off I'd have to run across four lanes of heavy traffic and vault, in a suitably dynamic fashion, the fence that ran along the central reservation.

It's only advantage as a location was that, should the stake-out become protracted, we wouldn't have to go far for refs.

'It's him, isn't it?' said Abigail as I got in.

'I don't know,' I said. 'Maybe.'

I handed Abigail a twenty and told her that she could either find a café on the high street to wait in or catch a train back to the Folly.

'You think he's the bad man?' asked Abigail when she saw the twenty.

'If it is him, I'm not comfortable with you being this close,' I said. At least not until I had a sprinter full of backup and/or Nightingale had arrived.

'There's a Greggs up by the station road,' she said. 'I'll wait there.'

'You sure?' I asked. 'It could be a long time.'

She held up a tatty hardback copy of *Tacitus: Histories I & II* in the original Latin. Judging from the dust jacket, a photograph of the Colosseum, it was post war and hadn't come from the Folly's library. Plus I had the Folly's only copy on a shelf in my room.

'Where did you get that?'

'Second hand shop,' said Abigail.

'You spent your own money on it?'

'Might have done,' said Abigail. And, when I didn't say anything, 'Miss Margot gave it to me.'

'What, Margot the Maggot?' I said. Miss Margot had been a teacher when I was at school. She'd taught RE[6] and I don't remember her as being all that encouraging.

'She's the one organising the GCSE for me.'

'You never said.'

'You never asked.'

'So how long has she been teaching you Latin?'

'You know when I asked whether you'd teach me magic?' said Abigail. 'And you said you would when I passed my GCSE?'

'Since then?' I said.

'Believe it.'

Oh, shit.

But at least it explained why she'd picked it up so fast.

'So you going to keep your promise?' she asked.

'We'll talk about it after,' I said.

---

[6] Note for Reynolds: Religious Education

'After what?'

'After we're done here,' I said.

Abigail nodded.

'Laters,' she said.

And the moral of that story is, think before you open your gob.

Which left Geoffrey Toobin who, had I not suspected he was either holding or had already murdered Brené McClaren, I would have regarded as the least of my current problems.

I had a good view of his front door, but there were windows around the back at ground level and our friend Geoffrey could have been hopscotching his way to freedom even as me and Abigail were saying goodbye.

Luckily Jaget turned up not five minutes later.

'Thames Valley have got a person of interest,' he said as he got in.

And it's obviously not Geoffrey Toobin, I thought, so I asked who.

'A Polish Barista,' said Jaget. 'Janusz Zdunowski.'

I asked why TVP liked him in particular and Jaget said that their canvass had led them to the Costa on the High Street where Brené McClaren was known to pop in on her way to work each morning.

'Wait,' I said. 'That's not on her way to the station.'

'No,' said Jaget and explained that Brené only started turning up for tea three months earlier – just a week or so after Janusz started work there. Not a coincidence, according to Janusz's fellow baristas, who had been taking bets as to how long it would be before Brené plucked up enough courage to ask him out.

'And Thames Valley like him for the abduction?' I asked.

'They like that they have CCTV footage of him and Brené chatting in the car park the morning she disappeared,' said Jaget.

The car park filled the space between the A416, which I was currently parked the other side of, and the pedestrianised High Street where the Costa was located. I asked how much CCTV they had and what it showed, but Jaget said that was all DS Transcombe had told him.

I said that whatever else, we needed to cover Geoffrey Toobin's back door and we settled who was going to leave the nice comfy car and loiter suspiciously around outside with a quick game of rock, paper, scissors – best out of three. Jaget always favours paper, but he hasn't figured out I know that yet.

While Jaget was getting into position I called Nightingale and briefed him. We decided his best option would be to drive to Aylesbury nick where the Thames Valley Major Investigation Unit had its incident room and where he could swing his rank from side to side and persuade TVP to take us seriously.

While he was heading across the Chilterns I got out my tablet and Googled Geoffrey Toobin until I had the address of his solicitor's firm and a confirmed picture of him. I risked a PNC check on his name and address – just because it's a small town doesn't mean there couldn't be more than one Geoffrey Toobin. He didn't have any previous, but he did have a driver's licence and registered vehicle – the Red VW Golf I could see parked, ironically, down a nearby side road.

Then I called up Abigail and asked her to trace a route

from Toobin's solicitor's office to Janusz Zdunowski's Costa and/or his house.

'But without going anywhere near the house,' I said. 'Or any Thames Valley Police that might be hanging about.'

Abigail told me not to worry.

I sent the picture of Geoffrey Toobin to Nightingale's phone and asked if he could try and persuade the MIU to add him as a nominal to their investigation.

I called Jaget and updated him. He kept me amused by complaining for five minutes solid, but alas even that had to end and I settled into my seat and awaited developments.

Abigail reported back that the fastest route from Geoffrey Toobin's office to his home ran past the Costa and then through the car park. I dutifully wrote this up in my notebook, but when I called Nightingale to update him his phone went straight to voicemail. Since with Nightingale this could signify anything from a loss of bars to full-on magical Armageddon I didn't find it at all comforting.

Abigail phoned to say she was heading back to town but I was to call her as soon as anything interesting happened.

A woman from the Chinese restaurant came out and asked if I could move my car. When I explained why I was there, she popped back in and brought me a full meal in a bag – crab with ginger and spring onions plus sides. This is why it always pays to try and park outside Chinese takeaways.

I watched the house across the road, chomped my way through the prawn crackers and wondered about the basement. It definitely wasn't big enough, but I hadn't spotted a second staircase or trap door and I'd been really looking. The later period brick bond of the end wall suggested that a section had been walled off in the nineteenth century, but despite the whitewashing I'd swear it was bereft of convenient secret doors.

I wondered whether there was a spell for detecting life at a distance.

Think how useful that would be as a skill for rescue workers. No more mucking around with infrared cameras and listening devices.

Could genius loci do it? Could Bev? I'd have to ask her. But even if she could, it might not be a conscious thing. Bev often talked about some things being a function of the river and some things being Beverley Brook, young woman about town, and that she didn't always know which was which.

'Like when you kiss me,' she'd said. 'Is it enjoyable because of the physical sensation or is it because you think it should be enjoyable?'

Good question, and we quickly developed experimental protocol which unfortunately left us too knackered to record our results properly and thus invalidated any conclusions. We have faith in the methodology, though, and continue to repeat the experiment on a regular basis.

And people say science is dull.

Someone rapped at my window and I started.

It was DS Transcombe – leering at me through the glass.

'Evening all,' he said and climbed into the passenger seat. 'Any movement?'

I said no, and nothing from Jaget around the back neither.

'Your weirdo governor is going to be along in a minute, accompanied by my totally normal and not in any way peculiar governor,' said DS Transcombe. 'And some bodies and a POLSA.'

I asked what had happened to the Polish Barista.

'We like your guy better,' said DS Transcombe. 'Especially now we have CCTV of him harassing Brené McClaren outside Costa.'

'The day she vanished?'

'At least three incidents over the two weeks previous,' said DS Transcombe. 'We think he tried to follow her home on the last occasion.'

Shit, I thought, classic stalker escalation.

'Here they come,' said DS Transcombe as a very dodgy-looking white Hyundai pulled up outside the parsonage with a couple of unmarked Astras in tow. Nightingale and another man got out of the back of the Hyundai. The second man was white, stocky, with brown hair in a buzz cut and a loosely cut black suit.

This was the SIO Detective Inspector Vincent Colombo, said DS Transcombe.

'He loves having people make jokes about his name,' said Transcombe. 'So feel free to pile in when introduced.'

Nightingale and Colombo stood aside as an entry team formed up, a couple ambling round the back to join Jaget. I went to get out, but DS Transcombe told me to stay put.

'You're the Falcon reserve, apparently,' he said.

They started with a bell ring, a police knock, then a fist bang accompanied by shouts of 'we're the police' which was then bellowed through the letterbox. I saw Colombo ask Nightingale something and when he answered they both turned to look back across at me.

Colombo called us on DS Transcombe's airwave.

'Are you sure he's still in there?' he asked.

I said as sure as I could be.

There was more discussion across the road and one of the uniforms donned a riot helmet and gloves before pulling the big red metal key from the boot of one of the Astras. There was a bit of a shuffle as they all lined up behind him before he swung the business end of the key into the door and it banged open as sweet as you could want.

They all trooped inside.

'Got any snacks?' asked DS Transcombe.

I was just about to hand him the emergency stake-out bag and let him take his chances, when his airwave squawked and a voice that identified itself as the DI gave the address and requested an ambulance.

'I have a male with life threatening injuries, wounding to wrists, unconscious but still breathing.'

So, suicide attempt.

'I have sufficient units on the scene at the moment – I will post a PC on the door to meet SCAS.'

SCAS to me was the serious crime analysis section of the National Crime Agency.

'SCAS?' I asked.

'South Central Ambulance Service,' said DS Transcombe.

The airwave squawked again.

'Grant,' said the DI. 'Inspector Nightingale wants you in here now.'

8

The Master's Palace

Geoffrey Toobin died in the ambulance.

Later examination determined that he had slit his own wrists while lying fully clothed in a bath full of warm water. You can never be totally precise, but it was estimated that he must have run the bath as soon as I'd left the parsonage.

'He knew I knew,' I said.

'Yeah, but what did you know?' said DI Colombo.

'Obviously something,' I said. 'If only I knew what it was.'

The simplest theory of the crime was that Geoffrey Toobin had drugged Brené McClaren, stashed her in the basement, murdered her, probably in the basement, then disposed of her corpse in one of the many convenient body-dumping sites afforded to those who live in the outer suburbs. Then he'd cleaned out the basement and scrubbed every surface as a forensic counter measure.

'Then you turn up on his doorstep,' said Colombo, 'he loses his composure and ends it all.'

He had officers out doing door to door and at Geoffrey Toobin's office trying to timeline his activities back from now to the day before Brené McClaren went missing.

There were no obvious signs of a second basement,

but a house as big as the parsonage would have had one matching the area of its ground floor. I have my artistic limitations, but even I can draw a rectangle and measure its sides. And I estimated that the current basement only covered one third of the potential area. It wasn't much but it was enough, with Nightingale's help, to get Colombo and DS Transcombe down into the basement.

'And you think there's another room behind that wall?' said Colombo. 'And that Brené McClaren is in there?'

'It makes sense from an architectural standpoint,' I said.

'But there's no door,' said Colombo. 'Or any sign of recent brickwork.'

'That we know of,' said Nightingale.

'And you want to pull down the wall?'

'If she's dead, then we can wait to pull it down slowly,' I said. 'But if she's still alive . . .'

'Do we have any reason to believe she is?' asked Colombo.

I considered telling him that Alice Bowman, even more late than late of this parish, had intimated that the 'princess' still needed rescuing. You know how sometimes things sound better in your head than when you say them out loud – this line didn't even sound good in my head.

'Information received, Vincent,' said Nightingale, who was allowed to call strange DIs by their first name. 'The same information that brought this case to light in the first place.'

Colombo nodded slowly.

'Fine,' he said. 'We'll have to get some workmen down here, then.'

'That will not be necessary,' said Nightingale, adjusting his cuffs. 'If you'd like to stand back?'

'And turn off your mobile phones,' I added.

The last time I saw him do this spell I was a bit distracted, what with the shotguns and the imminent fear of death and everything. The trick, Nightingale told me later, is being precise with *inflectentes*, the sub-formae that change the way the principal forma acts upon the material world. Also, the last time he done it he'd done it fast – this time it was slow enough to watch.

Nightingale made a short chopping motion with his hand. There was a loud crack and dust sprang from a split down the midline of the wall from ceiling to floor. The open hand became a fist and the bricks along that line twisted outward and the greyish brick dust fountained out as they ground noisily against the mortar trying to hold them in place.

Colombo and Transcombe took an involuntary step backwards.

'Bloody hell,' said Colombo.

When the line of bricks had all turned out ninety degrees, Nightingale paused to let the dust settle.

He told me to see if I could see anything.

I sidled up to where the twisted bricks had left a gap up the centre – it looked like a gigantic, half-open zip. I touched one of the bricks – it was warm under my fingers. Friction, I wondered, or an interaction between it and the force that moved it?

'Peter,' said Nightingale. 'If you wouldn't mind . . .'

I tried various points of view, but even with light leaking in from my side all I could make out were angular shadows in the darkness.

But there was the acrid winter bedroom smell of old sweat, breath and ancient farts.

I stood back and said I couldn't see anything.

'But there's definitely somebody in there.'

'Alive?' asked Colombo.

'Let's find out,' said Nightingale.

His fist twisted and I felt the power as the smell of white willow and mown grass, as the sensation of rough wool and a young voice singing something choral – high and sweet.

And behind it the impression that I stood amidst the precision gears of a vast clockwork orrery – smoothly and patiently reordering the cosmos to match its creator's design.

Give him a place to stand, I thought, and I believe he could move the world.

He certainly made short work of the wall.

I watched as bricks divided like a herd of sheep and bounded left and right to form neat piles in the corners of the room. Dust rolled over us and I had to cover my mouth with my hand. Back at the Folly I have filter masks and eye-protectors for just this eventuality.

Nightingale flicked his hand with an almost negligent gesture and the dust cloud parted like a curtain. A last few stray bricks clunked down onto their piles.

'Light, if you will, Peter,' said Nightingale.

I conjured a nice low powered yellow werelight which revealed the space beyond the now missing wall. For a moment I thought we'd uncovered nothing more than a hidden wine cellar, but the shelves that lined the aisles were the wrong size and the glass vessels they held were shaped like small demijohns.

There were three aisles between the shelves and behind the leftmost one a woman was stretched out on the floor, lying on her side, head resting on one out-stretched arm. Nightingale surged forward, stopping beside her to check pulse and breath.

'She's alive,' he said.

Colombo snapped his fingers and sent DS Trans-combe running up the stairs.

The paramedics had been on standby upstairs and as they came thumping down the steps I moved into the centre aisle to avoid my werelight messing with their equipment and had a closer look at the individual jars. Most of them were filled to the neck with a cloudy liquid, although some had visible cracks and were empty or part drained. I tapped a couple with my fingernail – cautiously, just in case there was a facehugger lurking inside.

I could hear the paramedics in the next aisle lifting Brené McClaren onto a stretcher. Their voices were un-hurried and lacking the urgent edge that is the harbinger of bad news at the scene of an accident.

A flicker of light at the far end drew me up the aisle. At first I thought it was a reflection of my werelight, but as I approached I saw it was a genuine glow from inside the centremost jar. I reached out and placed the tips of my fingers against the cool, green glass.

And I was for a moment in a palace of glass, standing on a formal lawn bounded on all sides by shifting planes of crystal. Standing before me was a man in a velvet frock coat whom I later identified, from the portrait hanging in the billiards room at the Folly, as George Buckland.

'You have certainly been tardy,' he said.

'Your messengers went a bit astray,' I said. 'Are you the only one left?'

'I am, and soon to be also quit of this wretched existence,' he said. 'I follow on to whatever undiscovered country they have found.'

I wanted to ask how the jars worked to trap ghosts, to ask whether there was a continuation of consciousness, and to see if I could determine whether the ghosts in the jars were really people or not.

But it was too late. The light was fading, and with it any sense that I was anywhere else but standing in the cellar of a house in Chesham. Still, as he went I was pretty certain that George Buckland, Master of the Glass Palace, looked me straight in the eye.

'*Vita non est vivere sed valere vita est,*' he said – Life is more than merely staying alive.

And then he was gone.

9

The Refugee's Daughter

And that was that.

Thames Valley Police were happy – kidnapper identified, victim saved, Operation Polygon resolved in less than thirty-six hours. Good bit of heart-warming media coverage and the clear up rate enhanced. Beer and commendations all round, thanks for the help boys, don't let the ticket barrier hit you on the way out.

We still had no idea what inspired Geoffrey Toobin to kidnap Brené McClaren. He didn't leave behind a note, diary or even a creepy vlog. There might be stuff on his laptop, but TVP technical forensics were holding that and cracking it is not exactly a priority job. From a policing perspective, motive is always less important than means and opportunity.

Who knows why anybody does anything, right?

But I couldn't help wondering what effect sleeping night after night over that basement full of concentrated ghosts might have had on Geoffrey Toobin. Abigail has dug out the archives and George Buckland and his grandson Walter weren't the firmest pair of bananas in the bunch, even before they had themselves walled into a cellar. TVP actually found their bodies in separate niches behind the jars, and there was a brief moment of panic that Toobin had been a serial killer until the pair were dated and turned over to the archaeologists.

Abigail thinks they were looking to extend their lives by becoming preserved ghosts themselves. Judging by the Latin George quoted as he went, it hadn't been a total success.

Once Brené McClaren was fit enough to be interviewed, she confirmed that she'd picked up her tea from Janusz Zdunowski, then, feeling strange, she'd allowed herself to be led out into the car park at the back. We have CCTV of Toobin in the Costa with Brené on that morning and he's close enough to slip something into her tea. We can't prove it, but we reckon that must be what he did. Brené loses track of events in the car park before coming to her senses in a strange, brightly lit basement.

She confirmed that when she was held there, there had been a camp bed with sheets and a duvet as well as a bottle of Evian and a Tupperware sandwich box complete with sandwich. Brené said that she had no doubt what had happened to her, and so disassembled the camp bed to yield a suitable club to beat the shit out of whoever her kidnapper was as soon as he came through the door.

Only he never did.

Brené's last clear memory was of sitting up against the far wall of the cellar and trying not to fall asleep. By the time TVP allowed us to conduct a separate Falcon follow-up interview, the memories of what happened next had obviously started to fade.

'I think I dreamt about Alice in Wonderland,' she said. 'There was tea on the lawn and a girl dressed in a Victorian costume. In fact everybody was dressed in costume. No, sorry, it's gone. I wasn't scared, though, I just remember being puzzled by a strange sound.'

We asked about the sound and she said it was like that fluting you get when you run a finger around the rim of a wine glass.

She assumed that she went to sleep still leaning against the wall.

And that wall is another thing that bugs me.

I know recent brickwork when I smell it and I'd swear that that cellar wall had been intact for at least a hundred years. In which case, how did Brené McClaren escape into the glass palace? If there was a secret door that I missed, then the evidence was obliterated when Nightingale went all 'Hulk smash' on the wall. And if she teleported or dimension-shifted or whatever, I don't even want to think about what that does to our understanding of the nature of reality.

And even if I did want to think about it, it wouldn't help me with my detective exam.

We have the rose jars in boxes downstairs in a disused servants' room near the armoury. Me and Nightingale had to do the clearing out ourselves because obviously we didn't want any random builders knowing the layout of the Folly's basement. Molly provided tea and moral support, Frank Caffrey fitted the smoke detector, helped drink the tea and made sarcastic comments about how level the shelves were. Harold Postmartin, our archivist, promised to see if he could dig out any additional references to the jars or to catching ghosts in general from the semi-secret stacks at the Bodleian.

Abigail wrote a report on George Buckland, his descendants and their Ghost Palace which I couldn't read because it was in Latin. Harold read it and agreed that it was excellent Latin and if only the current crop of undergraduates at Oxford conjugated half so well.

'Cicero would have been beside himself,' he said.

Abigail crossed her arms and gave me a hard look.

Just under two years ago I'd stupidly said that I'd teach her magic when she passed her Latin GCSE, and according to Harold this was A-star A-level standard at the very least.

As Nightingale says – 'Sometimes it's wise not to take the craft too lightly.'

We talked about it at the next magic boxing session – which is the traditional, manly way wizards are supposed to learn how to fling spells while avoiding being hit in the head.

'The time has come,' said Nightingale. 'To make a decision about Abigail.'

We'd both been avoiding this for at least three months, mainly because we didn't like the implications.

'Do we have to?'

'She's already cavorting with the mysterious and the uncanny,' said Nightingale. 'At the very least she needs to be able to protect herself.' And to further emphasise his point he attempted to impello me across the room. In response I did the patented Peter Grant shield shimmy, where you flick up a shield and angle it so the impello slides off. I like to combine it with a side step and a right hand jab.

It didn't land – I should have gone left instead.

'It's not our decision to make,' I said.

'If not ours, then whose?' said Nightingale 'We are

the responsible parties in this respect – we cannot evade it.'

'You're not getting me, boss,' I said. 'We both know that from the Folly's point of view she has to be trained but . . . it's her parents who are legally and morally responsible for her wellbeing. We can't usurp that authority – can we? And we can't just pretend it's one more youth activity. This is the craft, this is the forms and wisdoms – it's bare serious stuff.'

'You're right, of course,' said Nightingale. 'We'll have to make a full disclosure and explain the risks.'

I asked how it was done in Nightingale's day, and unsurprisingly found that it was assumed that a chap's parents already knew what it was they were sending their children to wizards' school to learn. He admitted that those rare types that took up an apprenticeship in their teens did so with the consent of their parents – or at least their father, which in those days was deemed to be the same thing.

'Do you want me to do it?' I asked.

'Good Lord, no,' said Nightingale. 'Much as I appreciate the offer.'

*

So, having slipped out of one ethically complex task, it was time to address the baby elephant in the swimming pool.

I had done my due diligence – there were no missing children of the correct age and description reported anywhere in the UK that could have turned up on Allen and Lillian Heywood's back garden on the night in question. Not even if we assume they were snatched as babies and kept somewhere else until that night.

I entertained the possibility that Chess might have been smuggled in from Eastern Europe. But, if so, how could I prove it? I was going to have to find a way to bureaucratically normalise his relationship with the Heywoods, which wasn't going to be easy. Getting the permissions for Abigail's one-girl youth club had taken most of a week and a couple of ethically questionable acts of magic to facilitate, but proved that sort of thing was doable with application of sufficient juice.

Which left the fact that Allen and Lillian were raising a young river god with no earthly idea of what they were about. They needed some support both physically and spiritually, and fortunately I had a notion how to get it.

So I took my favourite goddess to see Chess who, I was pleased to note, was properly awed to be in her presence. For about two seconds . . . before he grabbed her hand and started to drag her through the house, out through the garden and towards his river. Beverley allowed herself to be dragged, although she did pause to strip down to the Cressi Termico swimsuit she was wearing under her clothes. It always pays to anticipate.

Allen and Lillian followed us out into the garden in a worried huddle and then stared mutely at me – waiting for an explanation.

'Don't worry,' I said. 'This is perfectly normal.'

'Is she from social services?' asked Lillian.

There was a double splash behind me as Bev and Chess went into the river.

'Think of her as part of a support group,' I said.

'Does she know how to swim?' asked Allen, starting to look worried. 'Only they haven't come up yet.'

'Absolutely,' I said. 'Brilliant swimmer.'

'How long are they going to stay down?' asked Lillian with rising panic.

'Until they get bored,' I said.

There was a long pause.

'So, how about a cup of tea,' I said. 'And maybe some of those nice teacakes?'

Technical Note

There was no third parsonage at Chesham although the history of the split advowson is broadly true. High & Over House is a real place lived in by real people so if you do go and have a look do not disturb them. The foxes are keeping an eye on the place so I'll know if you do.

**Turn the page for an
interview with Ben Aaronovitch**

Hello, I'm Paul Stark from Orion's audio team and I'm delighted to be joined today by Ben Aaronovitch, author of the bestselling *Rivers of London* PC Peter Grant series, available in hardback, paperback, ebook and audio narrated by Kobna Holdbrook-Smith. Ben, welcome, we're here to talk about London and magic today. How are you doing?

I'm fine, thank you. Very nice to be here.

Fantastic. Well, on to a simple question to start with: What drew you to write about London?

I always find this a very strange question. I'm from London. Should I write about Birmingham, you know? I write about London because it's my home town, and I'm lazy and don't like to go outside the M25. It's what I know. I'd like to see more books – urban fantasy books – set in places like Birmingham – especially Birmingham, which I think is a very neglected city – and places like that and learn about those places. But all the people from those places seem to come to London and write books about London.

So, perhaps maybe the question you should ask is 'why do you write?' I write about London for a very simple reason: I'm a Londoner. I'm not sure why Neil Gaiman and David Carey and everyone writes about London, except for they've moved here and now they write about it.

And it's an amazing city. Lots of history, wonderful characters and myth that kind of provides a bedrock for fiction. What prompted you to add magic?

It never occurred to me not to add a magic. This is another one of those questions that's rather like saying to a man that has set out to do a long walk, 'What prompted you to use your feet?' What prompted me to use my feet – I thought: I want to do magic cops. That was the first thing that came into my head. So, really, the magic is built in. Magic cops implies magic right from the start. So, really, the rest of that was kind of detail. So, we're going to start with the idea that we're going to have policemen who do magic and then everything else was a question of who they are and what they are doing. Police who do magic in London was the starting point of the series and so I wasn't prompted to put magic into it, it was there right from the start. There were several things built in right from the start.

Given that you've also told us that you should 'write what you know', is this your way of telling us that you can *actually* do magic?

No, I am, in fact, a total sceptic. However, magic is *a lot* of fun to write about. So I can't do magic. Honest.

What made you go beyond the magic cops? To make the rivers one of the key bases? Was it something you knew about, something you were passionate about?

No, I didn't actually know that much about the rivers. I came up with the idea of Mama Thames for a different project and then I incorporated elements of another project in the initial idea and then for the book. And once you have Mama Thames and look at a map of all the tributaries, you just go 'ooh, they must all be stroppy women'. So that's where they came from. And if you just look at them you can just see their personalities; a lot of them you can just see their personalities from looking where their courses are. So, you know Fleet, you know Tyburn, you know what they're going to be doing.

Are there any that you feel that you haven't written yet that you're really keen to?

Oh, there are tons! There's the River Rom, who is the goddess of illegal street racing. There's the Wandle, who, for historical reasons, is the goddess of used clothes shops and schmutter. Basically the goddess of schmutter. That's the Wandle.

Any beer connection? You've got a lot of breweries along the Wandle.

Possibly, possibly. The Wandle was a very popular river for industry, so you have the Romantics all setting up their factories down there. What are they called? I've forgotten their names. That's terrible. You know the people who believed in fabric for the masses and beautiful – you see this is the trouble. I do all this research and it all goes in one ear and out the other. People expect me to remember little details of Fleet's course, 'Does the Fleet's course—?' I don't know! I've got to look at my map to know these things. 'Where does Wandle . . .?' Anyway, there's a ton. There's a place called Black Ditch and I haven't really worked out where she fits in, and there's Hackney Brook and there's all the history of the Lea – a very complicated river as anyone who has ever looked at a map will tell you. And so there're tons of people. You know I'm going to be writing for millions of years before I get to the end of the rivers and that's not even counting going upstream and the Ash and all those. So . . .

Lots of scope.

Lots of scope.

You mentioned earlier one of the prospects of writing on Birmingham. Now, I realise I'm asking a very geeky question here, but would each canal have an individual spirit?

I don't know. I'd have to go to Birmingham and find out. I don't know, I'm trying to avoid the idea that everywhere has a spirit, a genius loci. Really the question is: would it be fun if it had a genius loci? So, Grand Union Canal has a genius loci. I didn't mean it to have a genius loci and had no plans for it to be a genius loci and then I wrote a short story and it ended up having an orangutan for a genius loci, and it was like, 'I didn't plan that!', but you know . . .

Stories have a life of their own.

They often just go places I'm not expecting. So, yeah, I wouldn't like to say what would happen if I went to Birmingham because you're shaped by the environment you're writing in and therefore you go somewhere and you find things. That's the whole point of going somewhere is you find interesting things. There's no point in saying 'I'm going to do this' and then you go somewhere and do it, or, at least, there's no point for me to do that. It's much more fun to go somewhere and then have a look around and go 'ah' – you've got to smell the place, really. I always say that you've got to smell the streets before you can write about them.

Fantastic, fantastic.

Except the countryside, which always just smells the same.

There's a bit of a different smell depending on what the local livestock is, but yes.

Yes, unless you go downwind of a pig farm in which case it smells like 'Get the f— out of here'.

So, back on to your magic cops. Peter himself isn't great at magic, certainly he's been slow on the uptake somewhat. Do you find—

I love this notion that Peter is slow on the uptake.

Well, he's not slow on the uptake in general, but he certainly has perhaps been slower to develop magic.

Than who?

Than certainly Lesley, I'd say.

Are you sure about that?

I feel like I'm being led down a blind alley.

No, I mean this is where you get this weird idea from fanon, where *fanon* says Peter is slow at magic, slow at picking up magic. I haven't said if Peter is slow at picking up magic because apart from anything else Nightingale is a terrible teacher that way, with telling people how they're doing. No, Peter is as good as you would expect him to be – someone who has only been doing it for four or five years you know, under the conditions like that he's got two jobs. Remember he's also a police officer also doing all these cases, occasionally having buildings dropped on him, so he's not devoting his full time to it. So I think he's doing all right.

So, did you always envision that Peter would be a student, but dealing with Nightingale who is a phenomenally adept magician, but is terrible at teaching as you say? Was that always how you saw the dynamic?

Ah, well, Nightingale is very limited. I wanted to avoid Dumbledore. I wanted to avoid Gandalf. So, whatever Nightingale is, he's not Gandalf and he's not Dumbledore. He's not a teacher. He's not a mentor character. He is not, as by his nature, a mentor. He's not the wise man who tells you what to do. He's basically Hannay from *The 39 Steps*, he's basically Bulldog Drummond with magic. He's like a magical Bulldog Drummond, he's possibly the most powerful wizard that the Folly has ever produced in terms of being able to do stuff but ask him how it works and he's like 'Uh . . . you know, I don't know how it works. I just do it. I learn the formulas and am just good at it and can do these spells that no one else can do.' And he can do them quietly and he can do them fast and silently and all sorts of things. It's like he was good at sports except the sport was magic. He's basically that, he's one of those. I always imagine him in his cricket whites at Easterbrook: 'Argh, play the game!' or playing rugby, or the equivalent of rugby, and just charging through, you know, like 'rraaaawwgh' and snoozing through the academic part of the curriculum. So, you see, he's that guy and part of the reason that he has to look things up to teach Peter is he can't remember what he was taught and he has to go back. But he is very very good. He is excellently good, but in some ways this is almost a story about the limitations of power. So there's a limit to what you can do. If he got shot in the head from a distance he's buggered. You know, as he said, 'Shoot me. If you want to stop someone with my skills, just shoot me from a distance with a rifle.' There is a limitation. I didn't want — he can rip up a house by its roots and fling it over a garden fence, but he's not Superman. He's not a superhero. He has these limitations and magic has these inherent limitations. It does obey the rules of thermodynamics though it does bend them quite severely occasionally. Ultimately, the power has to come from somewhere and it can get dangerous if you overdo it.

Is that one of the reasons you've kept the top end of Nightingale's abilities somewhat under wraps? Ultimately he needs to be careful how much he exerts himself, how much he keeps from the public.

Well, there is that. There's also that he hasn't needed to. And also, the more difficult spells and subtle ones like actually putting Toby to sleep in the first book – that was one of the most powerful spells he's ever done in front of us, so to speak, in front of us in the book. Actually it's a very difficult spell. Peter's not going to learn that spell for like five years. Putting a dog to sleep. And Nightingale could probably put a person to sleep although he'd have to concentrate. You see, that sort of thing is very very hard. I've just written a passage in *Lies Sleeping* which discusses this, where Nightingale is doing something incredibly hard and Peter is astonished and it totally is a very simple thing. It's not complicated at all. See, in a way smashing things is easier.

It's almost like it's that much more difficult to accomplish good sleight-of-hand right in front of someone sitting with you than perform a big stage illusion.

Well, it's also that most of the subtle magic involves affecting people and people are very resistant to being affected. If you want to have a fight with someone you tend to just throw something at them, or you knock them down, or you pick them up and you throw them away. But human beings – in the way my magic is constructed – are very resistant. You can't reach into them and stop their heart. Magic is very bad at that. So, things like the glamour when you affect someone's mind – those are all really difficult to do. To make someone pick something up, to take control of their hand – that's really difficult to do.

The other side of that is that you've made magic and technology really incompatible as well. Why did you decide to do that?

Well, you have to explain why no one's recorded it on their mobile phones, don't you? Otherwise why aren't we looking at people, why is there no footage of Covent Garden, why is there no footage of half the things that have happened? Because it melts the chips. That's the reason I did it. Because you've got to explain why it's secret, otherwise it wouldn't be secret.

Once you'd made that decision and written that in had you thought about taking it further? What would happen if someone tried to do a spell on a flight for example?

You wouldn't. That would be a very bad thing to do. Unless it's a DC-3 you don't want to be doing spells on a plane. I've considered doing a scene where you have some of the most powerful wizards assembled and none of them can actually use any magic because they'd all kill themselves if they do. Nightingale probably could. Nightingale is so controlled that he could probably get away with it. But most things about technology – it's the chips, not the technology. Microprocessors are particularly vulnerable to magic. So, you're all right if you're running valves and stuff. Nineteen-fifties Russian technology would be fine. You could launch a Vostok and you wouldn't have to worry about doing magic with that, but not anything with a microprocessor, which is everything: your washing machine, your toaster, your cooker. And there's nothing mystical about it. There's good, solid world-building reasons why this happens. I built that in right from the start, but we may never find out what that is because the point is Nightingale doesn't know and I think Abigail, with forty years of study, might be able to explain it to you, although you wouldn't understand the mathematics of why it affects microprocessors. And I did that on purpose so that I would never have to explain it.

We've already touched on Birmingham, but are there any other cultures and their particular brand of magic that you'd like to explore?

I'd like to explore all of them! That's my big problem in life: that you cannot just do that. It's not really a question of cultural appropriation, which is what you essentially do when you're ignorant or you're knowledgeable but don't care. If you're honest, you can show what a culture is like, ask what a culture is like: What are the Chinese like at magic tied up with Daoism and stuff like that? But I just don't know enough Daoism to do that. It was quite hard to construct a magic system that was consistent with An-glo-Saxon and post-Norman, Roman Britain let alone one that's consistent with more than five thousand years of Chinese of continuous Chinese history, or Indian history, for that matter. You have thousands of years of culture in places like Africa and you have to say 'Can they do magic?' Everyone does magic, right? What Newton did in my world is he systemised it and created a system that Post Martin calls – ah, I can't remember what he calls it now, but he's got a fancy word for it: syncretism or something like that. He basically took it and systemised it and made it repeatable. He made it a science, basically. He took the things that people were coming up with by accident and he made it a science, because that was what Newton was like, that's basically what Newton did and why I chose him for the guy who did this: because he was interested. We know that. He wrote more about alchemy than he did gravity. We know he was as interested as anyone. As someone once said: if anyone was going to find out if magic was real it was going to be Isaac Newton so I figured, right, he did. That's the whole point. There is a reason why it's kept secret as well, but I can't talk about that.

Something to look forward to in a future book or inteview!

Yes, possibly.

You said you'd like to explore more. Is there anywhere outside London and the UK that you're currently researching with a view to writing?

Yes, I'm going to do a novella set in Germany. I don't think it's even going to be a Peter Grant book. Because this novella you're reading now was successful they want another one. And I thought that if I can't experiment with the novellas what could I experiment with? So, rather than taking a risk with a whole novel, I would like to write about Toby Winter who is essentially Peter's counterpart in Germany. I don't know why but he kind of turned up and started knocking on the door, like all my characters. I came up with this guy and I like him because he's slightly more lugubrious, he's more laid back than Peter in some ways. He's kind of fun, and also he's German so I've had to do quite a lot of research into how German magic works and all that stuff. And I've tried to stay away from recent history, stay away from the Nazis. Not because I feel like letting the German's off the hook or anything, but I feel you can ram that into the ground a bit. It's a bit like that occult Nazis have been done to death and with ignoring the history and stuff, like the Thirty Years War. Germany's a fascinating place, especially pre-unification Germany, when it's like a collection of states and you sit there going they're all Germans, but they don't think they're all Germans. It's a lot of fun so I'm looking into that for this story, which is going to be the next novella.

And will you be basing it around the rivers again? Will we be seeing the Rhine or the Rhone?

I don't know. Rivers of London is one thing, but I'm not sure you want to constantly go there. It's a bit predictable. 'Oh, look there's a river. Is someone in it? Oh, yes they are. Oh, it's Rhine Maiden.' We've established that the Rhine Maidens come visit the Thames for tips, so we know there are Rhine Maidens. It's not going to be the Rhine anyway, because it's going to be Trier. It's not the Rhine, but I'm going for a research visit soon, so I'll ask. Ask the river who she is, or it might be a him. You never know in Germany. Could be a guy. It's right on the border; I like it because it's right on the border with Luxemburg, so it's very liminal. It's one of those German cities that's changed hands quite a lot of times. It's also one of the oldest cities in Germany because it was established by the Romans and there aren't that many Roman cities in Germany. And wine. It's basically about wine. It's basically an excuse – I don't even like wine, but I can't resist this. I've basically just found a way of making it a claimable expense to get a wine tour of the vineyards of Trier.

That sounds like fun. I've a feeling I can predict your answer to this one because you touched on it earlier, but is magic purely fictional or do you think there are some elements of magic, or specifically your magic system that could be real?

You know what? I was born sceptical. I'm one of those people who didn't believe in Father Christmas when he was three and my parents tried, God bless 'em. But I make no claims of superiority. I've just go that kind of brain; I don't believe in any of it. I believe in coincidences. I believe that things happen by accident. A lot. I don't look down on people much who believe in stuff, but I just don't believe in any of it. I'm just really sceptical. Sorry.

Do you think that makes it easier to write magic?

Oh, god, yes! It's much easier to write because I'm not worried about whether it's accurate. I only have to worry about whether it's consistent, which is the classic thing in science fiction and fantasy. It's making what you do consistent. Unless – and this is very important – you deliberately don't. If you look at Jack Vance: he doesn't bother with consistency in his writing at all because he likes his magic wild and mad. I like consistency because essentially I'm a science fiction writer writing fantasy. I don't know how I ended up in this position, but it's how I ended up. But I do like a bit of wild magic, which is why I have the rivers. The rivers are my little bits of wild magic and they do wild things and strange things happen in the boundary of things. The fae are there and they're good for weird things happening on the boundary of things, but as for actual magic, no, I don't believe in any of it. I don't believe any superstitions at all. I just never have. It's not a considered intellectual position. I just never have believed in any of it.

How about the more human magic? Do you enjoy watching magicians work in sleight-of-hand and things like that?

Not particularly. I enjoy watching them work, if they're good, but I don't think to myself: 'Yay, magician'. I like Jonathan Creek. Does that count? I like the early two or three seasons.

As Tim Minchin said, Jonathan Creek is a bit like Scooby Doo because no matter how outlandish things get there's always an explanation for everything that makes sense.

Yes, that's part of the fun. It's much better. It's not doing it as old man Granger did it: In a mask, with glowy paint making glowing light.

And to go back to London for a little bit for one final question. We've touched a bit already on London's amazing history and the myths that have built up around

the city. Is there any particular legend or historical landmark or historical story that you're looking forward to building into a future Peter Grant mystery?

St. Paul's. St. Paul's is featuring very heavily in the book so far. I didn't mean it to, but in the same way the Royal Opera House became more and more important while I was writing the first one, St. Paul's has become more and more important while I'm writing the eighth one – oh god, I've lost track, seventh – it's the seventh. *Lies Sleeping*, anyway. The one after *The Hanging Tree*. And suddenly St. Paul's. I thought the climax was going to be in one place and now it's going to be somewhere else. And I thought it was going to be about one thing and now it's about something else and I'm sitting there going, 'Will you make up your mind!?' Which, of course, is futile. I'm arguing with myself. It's very schizophrenic, arguing with yourself. So, yes, I think that St. Paul's is going to get an airing. But there's so much. You know . . . I haven't even done the Tower of London! It sits there like a big chunky block of history, just there. The Tower of bloody London waiting for me. There's everything from the Bazalgette sewer system – given that it's about the rivers of London, I didn't even scrape the barrel, the side of a wall, when I did *Whispers Underground*. I did a whole book about the underground and I barely touched on Bazalgette. There's all that kind of stuff. There's so much history. So much stuff, from the Romans to the continuing debate about whether people actually occupied the inside of the city or they didn't. I met a Romanist and they said, 'No, no. Of course people lived inside the city, we just haven't found the remains yet.'

Because we built all on top of it.

Yes, we continuously built on it for the last two thousand years and so it's hard to tell. I don't know . . . when Deloittes or someone needs a new headquarters no doubt we'll find out.

Well, Ben, thank you so much for your time today.

That's all right. It was my pleasure.